A REASON TO FORGIVE

A REASON TO LOVE SERIES: BOOK 3

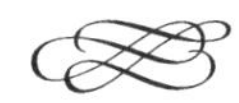

T.K. CHAPIN

WWW.TKCHAPIN.COM

Version: 12.12.2018

ISBN: 1791599737

ISBN-13: 978-1791599737

Dedicated to my loving wife.
For all the years she has put up with me
And many more to come.

CONTENTS

CHAPTER 1

CINDY DID NOT KNOW HOW to fix her marriage, but she knew it needed to change. Things between her and her husband, David, had steadily gotten worse over the last ten years, growing even worse in the last five years since their only daughter, Melody, moved out of the house. While Cindy kept herself busy with painting and activities at the church, her husband only grew more distant as time went on by throwing himself into work. She found herself more alone with each passing year, and she knew her heart couldn't take much more. Though she wasn't as young as she once was, she still had dreams. She wanted to travel, see new places, and experience all that life had to offer. David, on the other hand, did not. He used to want those same things in life, but that was when they were younger, before her mistakes. Life's difficulties had seemed to harden her husband's heart and, with time, they had drifted apart, their love growing cold.

One early morning in September, Cindy poured herself a hot cup of coffee from the carafe in the kitchen and then proceeded into the sun room adjacent to the kitchen. Cindy and David lived out in the country, about fifteen minutes from Spokane in the little community of Mead, Washington. Their property was down an old dusty dead-end dirt road. The only sounds that could be heard there were of nature and the creek that wove throughout the property. The two of them loved their home, and the tranquility had been their primary motivation in buying the land and building ten years ago.

While standing in the sun room in the quiet of the morning with her mug of warm coffee, Cindy stared at the stark white canvas sitting on her easel. The canvas had been sitting there for three days now. She had already coated it in gesso, a white sealant put on the canvas in preparation of painting with oil-based paints. The canvas was ready for her brush strokes, for her next great masterpiece. But for Cindy, the hardest part of painting was always the beginning. Just like always, she held the vision of what she wanted the painting to become. This was always the hard part, but today was different. Today, she felt ready. Finally, she dipped the bristles of the paint brush into the wet paint on her pallet and began to spread the very first stroke of color across the blank canvas. Cindy lived in the shadows of all the other paintings that had come before, though she'd often question herself. *What if this one isn't as good?* The thought sent waves of terror through her being and plagued her with the urge to procrastinate.

She continued to stare at the canvas as she took deep drinks of her coffee. The heat traveled down her throat and warmed her insides, fighting off a bit of that morning chill and anxiety lingering in the room. *You can do it. Don't over-think it.* A moment passed, then she set the mug down on the small table that held her paints, pallet, and brushes. She took a seat on the stool. Tilting her head, she let her eyes wander the sea of white and tiny splash of color, relaxing every muscle in her body as she attempted to prepare herself emotionally and physically to paint. Conjuring the image in her mind's eye, she took a deep breath. It was time.

"Cindy." Her husband, David's, voice broke into her concentration like a jack-hammer while a person is trying to sleep. Her determination melted away instantly, jostling her from the moment.

Without a reply, she turned toward him and raised a questioning eyebrow.

"Have you seen my favorite blue plaid long-sleeve shirt? I looked everywhere and can't seem to find it."

Disappointment rose up in her like flood waters rushing into a home during a storm. It wasn't so much the fact that he had broken her focus on the painting but that his interaction was the typical David. Void of love, and only seeking to satisfy himself. She often questioned what she was still doing with the man, then she'd remind herself of the vow she took before God and all their friends and family decades ago. She yearned for her husband to simply say things like 'Good morning' or 'How are you?' But that wasn't David, at least not anymore. She craved desperately for him to care. She wanted him to want her like he used to. He had been so caring, so understanding earlier on in their marriage and courtship. She couldn't change him, though. She knew that much. Cindy also couldn't switch off her feelings and desires like a light switch. And so, she lived with a constant ache in her heart as she longed for the husband and man she had married decades ago. Brushing her pain and self-pity aside, she raised her eyebrows as she thought of the usual spots around the house for his misplaced clothing.

"Did you check behind the door in the bathroom?"

"I'll check there. Thanks."

Then he left. *At least he said 'thanks' this time,* she thought as she turned back to the canvas. Pausing before refocusing, she prayed. *God, help me. I know it's all in Your timing, but I feel time is running out here. How long must I suffer through life unloved?*

Taking another drink of her coffee, she stared at the canvas as she recalled last month's art gallery event at the Civic in downtown Spokane. It was only the second event she had ever been invited to, and all the well-known local artists of Spokane were in attendance, but only six of those artists were requested to show pieces, and she was one of them. That evening, she sold her first painting ever. The sale was to a cute married couple she had only met that night, but she adored the couple immensely and couldn't have asked for a better first sale. Mr. and Mrs. Tyler Dunken. They lingered with her for hours, and the three of them spoke about art, faith, Diamond Lake, and how God works everything together for good. Cindy held a secret from them that night though. The whole time they were speaking about God working things for the better, she only thought about how her marriage felt like the exclusion to that rule. She loved the Lord just as much as any Christian in the pew on Sunday morning, but she didn't see how anything in her marriage was *good*.

After another half hour with her blank canvas and unable to re-focus, Cindy left the sun room and retrieved a load of laundry from the dryer. She headed to the bedroom with her basket full of procrastination and distraction. As she entered the bedroom, she saw David's wallet atop the dresser. Her heart flinched. *He probably needs that,* she thought to herself. Though she didn't like the way he was acting toward her in life, she still held a deep respect and love for the man. So, after she finished with the laundry, she grabbed the wallet and drove into town.

David was a part-owner and operator of Spokane's biggest restaurant supply company, *Carlton's.* He started the company twenty-four years ago with his long-time friend, Mark Johnson. Though they had a full crew and even trained managers on-site, they both involved themselves in the daily work. That was always David, though. He worked hard to provide for his family and Cindy did her best to respect that about him. However, it was hard for Cindy to have him gone so much of the time, especially after Melody was born. He took only one day off for her birth. Most weeks throughout their marriage, he worked over sixty hours. He made it home every night but had little time for much outside of reheating dinner, watching television, and then going to bed. Then, after Melody moved out five years ago, it was as if he did too. He started working more, and now she only caught small glimpses of her husband. Sometimes, it happened in the morning, like earlier that day, and sometimes right before bed for a few minutes. Outside of those moments, it seemed the only time she saw her husband was on their way to church, when Melody and her husband Tyson invited the two of them over, and when he was fading in and out in front of the television on the weekends. Cindy sensed a growing ocean of distance between their hearts and she felt utterly alone.

Arriving at the receptionist desk at *Carlton's Restaurant Supply,* Cindy raised her eyebrows as her gaze caught Jessica, one of the receptionists.

"He's not in. Out to brunch with the guys and Mark."

"Oh." Cindy's countenance fell, knowing she'd not be able to see him to return the wallet. Fishing the wallet from her purse, she handed it to Jessica. "He forgot this at home. Can you get it to him?"

"Yes, Mrs. Carlton. I'll get it to him."

As Cindy walked out of the establishment and headed

toward her car in the parking lot, a small cool September breeze brushed across her whole body, sending a chill to her core. Her aloneness crept into her bones and a wave of sorrow washed over her. Admittedly, she had hoped to see him for a brief few extra minutes today. Now that chance was gone. She got into the driver seat and prayed. *God . . . despite my sins, You love me. Despite my past, You accept me. Despite me, Lord, You died on the Cross for the salvation of my soul. I have no right to approach You, considering the mistakes I've made in this life, but I am coming to You. I am asking You to help my hurting heart. Please? It'll take nothing short of a miracle for David and me to return to the love and relationship we once had, but I know with You, all things are possible. Amen.*

Hot tears of hopelessness burned as they escaped the corners of her eyes and ran trails down her cheeks. Would she ever have her husband's loving arms back around her? Or was this it?

Her phone rang a moment later in the car. The number was local, but not in her phone book.

"Hello?"

"Hey, it's me, Olivia. From the gallery. My husband and I bought your painting."

Her sense of loneliness loosened in the moment and she was able to smile. "Oh, hey! I was just thinking about you and Tyler this morning! Did you guys settle on a spot in the house for the painting yet?" The night of the gala, after they purchased the painting, Olivia and Tyler were going back and forth in conversation about the various locations in their home where they'd like to hang the art.

Olivia let out a laugh. "Yes! He caved and let me hang it in the foyer. Listen, the two of us received an invite over to the inn for a marriage retreat that our pastor and his wife are holding for this upcoming weekend. We wanted to know if you and your husband would like to join us?"

Cindy's heart leaped. "Yes!"

"Great, we'll see you there. David can go?"

"I'll talk to him about it and let you know for sure if we can go. What's the cost?"

"Nothing. It's free. They don't want to build barriers for people to be reached by God, so they're making it all free."

Her heart fluttered. She knew money would be a huge barrier for David. Though they had plenty of it, he wasn't one to spend without good cause and she knew he'd have resistance to the idea, especially if it were to cost him anything. "That's great! I'll be in touch, and thank you for letting me know about it!"

"You're welcome. I hope to see the two of you there! There are only five rooms at the inn, so it'll be pretty low-key."

Cindy wasn't much for crowds, so at hearing that, it only drove her desire to attend deeper. "That sounds so amazing! I'll call you tomorrow morning and let you know."

Hanging up with Olivia, Cindy glanced up at the ceiling of her car and smiled with tears in her eyes. *Thank You.*

CHAPTER 2

DAVID ARRIVED BACK TO HIS OFFICE from brunch with his associate managers and Mark at eleven o'clock that morning. He tossed his suede jacket onto the couch in his office and noticed his wallet sitting in the middle of his desk. He approached and read the sticky note Jessica had attached to it. His wife had dropped it off for him. He recalled reaching for it at brunch and how it felt to not find it there. He didn't like it. Sure, Mark had a company credit card he used to pay for the meal, but he felt a part of him was missing without it. Knowing his wife cared enough to bring it by brought a smile to his face. He picked the wallet up off his desk and placed it into his back pocket and then took a seat behind his desk. He wiggled his mouse to wake the computer screen.

He thought again of Cindy. He loved her a lot, more than any other woman on the planet, but what she had done to him was unforgivable in his mind and in his heart. She violated his trust seven years ago, and for that, he could never trust her again. They once shared an intimacy and love for each other that ran deeper than the undiscovered depths in the ocean. But everything had changed and for the worst. He didn't divorce her, though he had every right. Instead, he kept it going out of convenience. The tax write-offs, the social connections at church, and most importantly, his daughter, Melody. It would've crushed her if he left, and he didn't want to do that to his daughter.

Letting go of the mouse, David turned his attention to the picture frame on his desk. It held a photograph of his daughter and her new family, her husband, Tyson, along with their now three-year-old daughter, Alice. Melody was pregnant with his second grandchild now, and his heart couldn't be more filled with joy each time he thought about it. His little girl was a mom now, and a wife too. He longed in his heart for the years of yesterday, when Melody was a child and the time when he could trust his wife. Life was perfect. Even though they didn't have a lot of money in the younger years of *Carlton's*, they had God, they had love, and they had each other. What else was there? All that was enough for David, even if it wasn't for Cindy.

David often took strolls around the restaurant supply warehouse and asked himself the same question repeatedly. *Why wasn't our life enough for her? Why wasn't I good enough for her?* He'd look at all the workers, all the merchandise on the shelves, the entirety of the kingdom he had built. It was all for her, all for their family. She had destroyed everything good in his life by her one action. David had arrived financially to the place he had hoped for so many years. He had growing retirement funds that most people could only dream of, and he could purchase anything he wanted if he so desired, but it all didn't matter. He couldn't enjoy a penny of the blessings from God after he'd found out about Cindy's affair. Though it had been seven years since it happened, David hadn't let it go, and it was as if it had just happened in his heart. The betrayal was like a knife wound in his heart that never healed. In his grief and pain, he felt utterly alone.

His desk phone's intercom buzzed. He pressed the button to answer Jessica.

"Yes, Jessica?"

"You have a call on line one."

"Who is it?"

"Your daughter."

His heart warmed, and he smiled. "Patch her through."

"One second."

"Dad?"

"Hey, Mel. What's up?"

"Tyson and I were wondering if you and mom could come to dinner tonight? At seven?"

"Have you talked to your mother?"

"No, not yet. I figured you were best to talk to first. If you're too busy, then there's no point in asking her. Right?"

"Right. Well, if your mother is up for it, I am too. Hey, how is Alice doing with preschool?"

"Good. She's making friends and enjoying it so far. It's only been a few weeks, but it's been good so far. It's nice to have a little break for a few hours in the morning too! This baby growing inside me wants me resting way more than I had to with Alice. So, in the end, I think it's a win-win."

"That's great to hear, honey. Call your mom and check with her on dinner, but I'm sure we'll be able to come."

After hanging up the call with his daughter, David began to think about Cindy. He could predict almost every movement and action before it happened with that woman. She'd be using that car ride together tonight to gripe at him about being able to fit in a dinner with Melody but not able to get home at a decent time for her. The sad truth was that he loathed spending time with her. He deeply desired for things to be different with Cindy but didn't see how it was possible.

. . .

ARRIVING HOME at a quarter to six that evening, David tossed his keys on the counter in the kitchen and went to the refrigerator. Opening the door, he pulled a bottle of water out and took a swig. As he shut the door, Cindy was standing right there on the other side and he jumped. He spilled his water down the front of his button-up white shirt, drenching it.

Raising an eyebrow, Cindy crossed her arms. "I startled you?"

He nodded and set the water bottle down on the stove and grabbed the hand towel hanging from the oven handle to pat himself dry.

"I find it interesting that you can always find time for these little impromptu dinners to Melody's house, but you can never find your way home for dinner with me."

She didn't wait until the drive, which was surprising. He thought to himself, *I wonder what she has in store for the drive?* David's heart hardened at his wife's predictable and critical words. He set the towel down on the stove and his hard heart decided to be harsh and honest with his wife. "You ever think I *like* spending time with our daughter and her family?"

Her eyes lit with a fiery anger and she shook her head. "You're incredibly unkind! I wonder if Melody would like to know the truth about how you really treat me! Think she'd like it?"

Scoffing, David shook his head and turned his back toward her. His heart only hardened more with the threats. Attempting to ignore her, he patted more of the dampness from his shirt. His voice was soft as he spoke a vile reply. "Yeah, and I wonder how she'd feel about your stepping out with an art teacher from the community college."

"What did you say?" Cindy inquired, her words questioning but her tone accusing. She grabbed his shoulder and whipped him around to face her.

"You're lucky I'm not a violent person, Cindy."

She was quiet for a moment, her emerald eyes glistening with tears. Her tone shifted to a soft and hopeless one. "You're never going to let me live my past down, are you?"

The way his wife asked the question broke through small layers of hardness, slicing through the years of hurt. He didn't want the fact that he couldn't forgive her to be true, but there was no denying it. He couldn't get past the pain, and God knows he had tried. He didn't respond to Cindy this time but instead merely peered down at the hardwood floor in the kitchen. His insides ached, and he longed for a way through the maze of grief he felt trapped in, but he had no way out.

Cindy didn't say anything for a long moment. Eventually, she ended the conversation, or lack thereof, with a sigh and left the kitchen. David wandered into the sun room and flipped on the light switch. Seeing paint now on the canvas, he was happy to see she had finally started. As his eyes drank in his wife's brush strokes on the canvas, his heart ached as the scene clicked in his mind. A nature scene, but not just any nature scene. It was from a camping trip that they had taken to Idaho shortly after the two of them married over twenty years ago. He could recall the scene because they had a photograph of it lying in a box somewhere. He could still feel how that trip felt. He could sense how it felt to stand at that exact spot she was painting. Pebbles lined the shoreline of the still lake a few feet in front of them and nature was all around. David's eyes moistened as the painting penetrated a part of his soul, as he remembered all the love and happiness from that day too. *If only our marriage could be fixed,* David thought to himself.

"David." Cindy's voice was soft, carrying a gentleness that

continued to stir a deep part of him. He didn't turn to her but listened for her to continue. "David, I was invited to a marriage retreat and I want you to go with me."

His anxiety rose within him. He knew it'd be similar to the past experiences they had undergone with marriage counselors right after the affair. There would be a lot of talking, a lot of emotions, and worst of all . . . lots of forgiveness being encouraged. He had tried that road before, traveled down it a long time, and it never did any good.

David turned to face his wife, but when he did, he saw something in her emerald eyes that stopped him cold. He was gentle as he responded. "I'll think about it. When is it?"

"This weekend. Saturday and Sunday."

Anxiety levels inside him rose even higher. "That's in two days."

"I know it's short notice, but . . . if you have any desire to fix what's not right between us, you'll consider it."

Wow, how did she know I want that? he wondered as he took a moment to respond. "Okay. I'll let you know."

She left the doorway of the sun room. Turning back to the painting on the easel, he studied the painting a while longer, letting his mind relive the camping trip. He was happy then. She was too. *God, I want that for my marriage. I just can't see it being possible.*

ON THE DRIVE to their daughter's house, Cindy once again brought up the upcoming marriage retreat.

"Olivia was the one who called me about the retreat. Olivia and Tyler Dunken."

She paused for a long moment, appearing to wait for David to reply. He tried to place the names but kept coming up blank. "Oh, remind me who they are again?"

"I swear, you don't listen to anything I say!" Her dig at

him kindled his anger, re-hardening his heart. She continued, adding fuel to the fire. "They bought my painting at the gallery, remember? The gala you never came to. I came home all excited that night because I finally sold a painting. Oh, wait, that's right. You were too consumed with a re-run of a Super Bowl from the eighties. Maybe you remember my interrupting your TV watching?"

A forest fire ignited inside David. He burned with anger. "Exactly how much about our marriage did you tell Tyler and Olivia? Did they buy your painting out of pity because I wasn't there?"

She glared. "How dare you! I didn't tell them anything about our marriage! Then again, I didn't have to. Remember? You weren't there. That said plenty."

Her words were like a dagger as they slid right between his ribs and struck his heart. As his heart ached, his tongue was set on fire. "Don't sit here and try to guilt me, Cindy! I had to work, and I don't know if you know this, but those paints you love to use cost money, and that money doesn't grow on trees! They come from *actual* work. Yes, I was watching TV, but I work hard, and I deserve to relax after coming home from a hard day at work!"

"Oh, of course. You are the one who earns all the money, and all I do is sit around and spend it. Oh, please."

"No. You work around the house, I get that. You do a lot to keep things running smoothly, but I don't need to be made to feel inadequate as a husband because I didn't show up to your gala."

She turned toward David and held out her arms. "You are inadequate, David!"

Flashes of memories from when the affair happened cascaded through his mind. She used the word 'inadequate' quite often back then. "I've heard *that* before! You had to cheat on me to make me a better man. Isn't that what you said? You heading that direction again, Cindy? Huh?"

It was as if the air had been knocked out of her lungs. Cindy dropped her arms and sat back into her seat. She wasn't speaking now, but tears of surrender streamed down her cheeks. David welcomed the sudden silence. In that moment, David could sense he had crossed a line, but he welcomed the quiet they experienced on the rest of the drive to Melody and Tyson's house.

CHAPTER 3

IT WAS A NEW RECORD for David. He had brought up Cindy's past transgression twice in one day to her. She was beyond hurt. The part that pained her deeply in her heart was the fact that he hadn't let it go. She, on the other hand, had made peace with it and moved on. *Why can't David do that too?* She wondered. Often, she'd follow up that thought with, *Easy for you to say. He didn't cheat on you.* It killed her to know what she had done wounded him so badly. And each time he brought it up, it was like he was crucifying her all over again. Her heart was full of pain and she knew deep down that it was all her fault. If she hadn't cheated on him, none of the pain she had been reaping for years now would even exist. *Why'd you cheat?* It was a question she asked herself every day for a long time after it happened. All she could ever come up with when asking herself that question was that David didn't make her feel loved like he used to, and she was lonely. But she knew that wasn't true after he *really* stopped his affections for her after she had stepped out. *That* was true loneliness.

As they pulled into the driveway of Melody and Tyson's

house, Cindy put on her happy mother and wife face. If there was one thing good about David and Cindy's marriage, if you could call it *good,* it would be the fact that they looked like the perfect couple to the world. He was strikingly handsome for a fifty-year-old, and she didn't look a day over thirty-seven. Everywhere they went together, people would comment on how perfect they were for each other while secretly, they couldn't stand each other.

David turned to Cindy as he shut off the car. "Don't bring up the marriage retreat to Melody, please."

Undoing her seat belt, Cindy looked at David. Shaking her head, she let out a laugh. "You afraid she'll encourage you to go?"

"No, it's not that. It's just none of her business, and we don't need to involve our daughter in our relationship. You know what? I have an idea. Maybe you can give her and Tyson our spot at the retreat. Because I'm not going."

It was if David had cut the single thread that bonded their marriage together and it felt as if a deep splinter tore through her heart. Cindy got out of the car without a word and slammed the door. She expected him to get out shortly after, but he didn't. She turned and peered over her shoulder. She could see him through the windshield. David was sitting with a smile on his face and his phone up to his ear. He looked like he had no care in the world and everything was business as usual in his little world. It drove her mad. She glanced up at the evening sky as she looked away from him. *Why does he have to be the way that he is, God? Can't You smite him or something?* Finally, he hung up and got out of the car. As he joined her side, she felt a thought float to the tip of her mind. *Trust me.*

"I know you're a respecter of *feelings* and other people's *emotions."* David's tone of voice was joking and rude. He continued. "With that being said, my not wanting to go isn't a problem for you? Is it?"

"It doesn't surprise me that you don't want to go. Honestly, David, I don't think you could let me down any more than you already have." Her words were gentle, sad, and by the look in his eye, they struck a chord somewhere in that soul of his, if he had one left. Her gaze landed on the front door of their daughter's house. "Now can we go have a pleasant meal with our daughter as we pretend everything is fine?"

Curt in his reply, he nodded. "Yep."

"You have every reason to be mad at me for what happened in the past, David. But if that's how you really feel after all this time, then maybe it's not wise to be together. God permitted divorce for our hardened hearts, and maybe your heart cannot be softened."

"I never said I wanted a divorce." His expression was weighted, his lips in a frown, and worry lit in his eyes. He opened his arms up and turned toward her. "Is that what you want? A divorce?"

She shook her head. "No, not at all. I want *us* back, David. The way things used to be in the old days. You remember how fun life was back then? We were young and in love and crazy."

He laughed, smiling as he smoothed a hand over his face and leaned against the car. The tension in the air loosened. "We were a couple of young dumb kids with a whole lot of life ahead of us." Then, his face darkened a moment later. "But all of that doesn't matter, Cindy. That wasn't reality. What you did to me *is* reality, and I honestly cannot trust you. I don't know how to trust you."

It hurt to hear David reveal his heart out loud for the first time in years. She hadn't heard much of anything from the man, and now in this moment right before going inside their daughter's house for dinner, he was opening up. *Why now?* She wondered, not saying a word. With her silence came more words from David.

"I want to trust you, Cindy. I really do. I just don't see how it's ever going to be possible again." He held out his hand toward the driveway behind them. "Now do you want our personal life spread throughout all the world at some marriage retreat this weekend? Is that your idea of a good time? Is that going to help me trust you better if I hang out with a bunch of other married people?"

Fear wrapped her heart in chains. She didn't want that either. Her response to David came immediately. "No, I don't want the details of our relationship out in the world."

"Then this retreat might not be a good idea. Not just from my point of view, but yours too."

"I hadn't thought of it that way. Hey, it's past seven o'clock. Let's get inside to Melody and Tyson. We'll talk later. Okay?"

He nodded.

LEAVING Tyson and David to their talk about their investments, Cindy escaped the table and went into the kitchen to join her daughter. As she entered through the swinging door, she found Melody serving up dishes of ice cream into bowls. She was licking a glob of ice cream that had fallen onto her hand from the scooper. Seeing her pregnant daughter warmed Cindy's heart. It felt like only yesterday when she was pregnant with Melody, and now here Melody was, having a second child of her own.

Watching as her daughter slurped up ice cream that had fallen to the side of her mouth, Cindy let out a laugh.

Melody laughed as she threw her hair over her shoulder and glanced over at her mom. "Can't a girl enjoy a happy accident? Speaking of accidents, did I tell you about Alice getting a popcorn seed stuck in her nose a few nights ago?"

"Wow." Cindy wasn't amused but concerned. "How'd Alice get ahold of a popcorn seed?"

Melody's laughter subsided, and she focused on the task of scooping ice cream. Digging the scooper into the tub of vanilla, she shrugged a shoulder lightly. "I thought it was a silly moment."

"It is funny now that she's okay, don't get me wrong. I'm really glad she's okay, but I'm legitimately concerned why my granddaughter had a popcorn seed. Not even a couple of weeks ago, she fell and hit her head on the concrete outside your house and bled a bunch, you said. I never had these issues with you growing up, and it seems like Alice has a new injury or issue that occurs every time I see you."

Shoving the ice cream scoop into the tub of ice cream, Melody looked at her mother with moistened eyes. "It's never good enough for you. Is it? It wasn't good enough when I found out I was pregnant with Alice. You had to suggest naming the baby after Grandma Wilma. It wasn't good enough for you that we got a car seat, because it wasn't the 'top-of-the-line' one that you magically found on sale the next day. Nothing is ever good enough for you, Mom!"

Melody started to cry and folded into her palms. Shocked at the overreaction, Cindy didn't say a word. A moment later, Melody stormed out of the kitchen, the doors swinging back and forth on the hinges.

Cindy's gaze caught the scoop in the tub of ice cream as she contemplated her daughter's words. *Is nothing ever good enough for me?* Then a gut-wrenching thought surfaced, and it felt as if her heart began to actually bleed. *David wasn't good enough either.* Eyes glistening and heart aching, she closed her eyes and prayed.

"Cindy." David's voice interrupted.

She turned to see David standing in the kitchen, the swinging door behind him slowed to a stop. His face was lit with concern.

"I heard everything. It's not true what she said. She's just hormonal right now from the pregnancy."

He made his way over to his wife, passing the bowls of ice cream, and took Cindy into his arms. His warmth was an old friend she had longed for and missed greatly. As her husband held her close for the first time in a long time, he didn't speak a word, and she didn't dare either. His embrace felt like the home she hadn't known in years.

Then, after a long moment of nothing being said between the two of them, David pulled back from their embrace. He gently set her back to look her in the eyes.

"I'll go to the retreat. We don't have to air our dirty laundry to get it cleaned."

"Oh, *David*!" She leaped toward him and threw her arms around him. She felt in that moment as if a lifesaver from God had been tossed to her just as she was about to slip beneath the tow. Her cell phone's notification tone sounded from her purse over on the counter just then, and she released her hold on David to see who it was. It was her sister, Sarah.

Sarah: Can I come this weekend? I need out of this house.

Cindy immediately shook her head as she finished reading the text. "I can't believe it."

"What?" David inquired, walking closer to her.

"Sarah wants to come visit this weekend."

"Oh, shucks. That's a bummer." Sarcasm dripped from his lips.

Cindy laughed and shook her head again as she replied to her sister that they had plans and wouldn't be in town.

. . .

After a quiet time of ice cream at the dinner table together, Melody stood up and took Alice to bed. Seeing a chance to repair things with her daughter, Cindy excused herself from the table. Stopping her daughter in the hallway as she came out from Alice's bedroom, Cindy raised her eyebrows.

"Listen, Melody. I'm sorry about earlier."

"Okay, Mom." She crossed her arms and glanced away, a look of pain still on her face and glistening in her eyes.

Reaching out, Cindy touched her daughter's arm lightly. "I love you and you're a wonderful mom. You know that, I know that, and your father and husband know that. Everybody knows it."

"I know." She pressed a hand against her forehead as she let out a sigh. "I'm just feeling super emotional right now."

"What's going on?"

She hesitated, letting her hand fall to her side. Then she shrugged her shoulders. "We're moving."

"What? Moving? Across town?"

"No. Concord, New Hampshire. Tyson got a new job that pays really well there, and we're moving at the end of the month."

Opening her arms, Cindy hugged her. It was sad that she was moving, but she couldn't help but be happy for her daughter's family. Tyson had been hoping for a promotion with his work. They just didn't know when it'd happen or where it'd take them. Now it had finally happened after two years of waiting. The thought of not seeing her grandchildren broke her heart, but she couldn't let her selfish thoughts get in the way of this opportunity for them.

David and Tyson came upstairs and into the hallway. Tyson stared at Melody. "You told her, didn't you?"

"Told her what?" David asked, turning toward Tyson with a confused look.

"We're moving to New Hampshire. Tyson got his promotion!"

"Congratulations, Son." Patting Tyson's shoulder as David shook his hand, her husband's heartache was evident to Cindy.

Though she felt painfully worried about her pregnant daughter moving away halfway through her pregnancy, Cindy knew it was the right decision for Melody and Tyson. They'd be starting a new life in a new city, and support was what they both needed that evening. She and David both encouraged them and prayed over them as they discussed their moving plans late into the evening.

Walking out to the car to leave that evening, Cindy couldn't help but feel a measure of sadness lingering in her heart.

"You okay, Cindy?" David's question was a surprise, a movement in the right direction and the marriage retreat wasn't even underway yet.

She stopped at her car door and looked over at David over the roof. "You haven't asked me that in years, David. Are you okay?"

He glanced at their daughter's house, then back at her. "Hey. I'm trying here. Can you cut me some slack?"

"I'm sorry. I am just worried about Melody moving, and honestly . . . sad."

"She'll be okay. She has Tyson with her, and you know . . . she's grown up."

Cindy sighed. "You're right."

CHAPTER 4

THE NEXT MORNING WHEN DAVID awoke, he immediately noticed Cindy wasn't lying beside him. Getting up out of bed, he wrapped himself in his robe and went to find his wife. When he found her in the sun room painting, he paused before letting himself be known to her. He watched as she chose a color from the palette, then continued to study her as she carefully painted intricate white brush strokes into the sky, forming clouds instantaneously. David marveled at her ability, watching as life was painted into the canvas. Folding his arms, he leaned against the door frame and in doing so, he accidentally knocked the broom over.

She turned on her stool.

"What? You can't find your socks today?"

"No." He shook his head as he moved from the door frame and lowered his arms. He took a step closer toward her. "I was just watching you."

She set her paint brush down and turned fully around. "You're acting strange again. What's gotten into you?"

He shrugged. "I don't know."

Cindy's eyebrows shot up. "Now that's a phrase I don't hear you say very often."

He laughed lightly, his gaze gravitating back to the painting. "Thanks for dropping off my wallet yesterday. I felt a little lost without it."

"I knew you would, so that's why I did it."

His heart warmed at her caring words. He knew his wife loved him, which seemed to make things only more difficult when it came to the pain he couldn't let go of in his heart. How could someone who loved him betray him in the worst possible way? David took another step closer to his wife in the sun room. His heart pounded in his chest as if warning beacons were sounding. *She hurt you before. She can hurt you again.* David ignored his thoughts, pushing them away from himself and the moment. "Cindy, listen, I agreed to go last night because of what you said."

She appeared perplexed. "Remind me of what I said?"

"In the kitchen yesterday, you said, 'If you have any desire to fix what's not right between us, you'll consider it.' As I was sitting there talking to Tyson at the dinner table, I caught a glimpse of a picture of us from our wedding day hanging on their wall, then I heard the painful conversation between you and Mel. It came together in a way that convicted me and I knew right then that I needed this retreat. *We* need this retreat."

Cindy stood up from the stool and closed the distance between them, hugging him tightly. "You *do* love me, David."

Bringing his arms up slowly, he wrapped them around his wife as his insides ached and his eyes moistened. "Of course I do. I never stopped loving you. I only stopped showing it."

Wiping her eyes as they released from their hug, David thought about his conversation in the car in Melody's driveway last night. He grimaced.

"What's wrong?" Cindy asked.

"It's nothing, really. I just have a meeting with Mark today and I don't know what it's about. It's probably about the point of sale system he wants to buy. He's been hounding me about it for months. The one we have is fine, so I don't understand why we need to waste money."

"Ah."

"Yeah." David shook his head, then let out a quick sigh. "I'd better get ready and go in. I'll try to be home for dinner tonight. Okay?"

She smiled. "You're already trying harder than you were, and we haven't even gone to the retreat."

He laughed. "I know. I think I'm just getting into the mindset of working on us. You know?"

Cindy nodded, beaming as she did. David loved seeing his wife smile, but he couldn't shake the worry. Could a retreat fix them? He had his doubts, but he also had hope now.

ARRIVING in the board room where Mark requested to meet that morning, David poured himself a glass of water from the pitcher and sat down in one of the high-back board-room chairs to wait. Mark spent a grip of cash to build that special board room and it was hardly ever used. Throughout the twenty-four years of being in business together, Mark had always been the spender, while David had been the saver. Many of Mark's decisions annoyed David, but he understood they brought the correct mixture to the table and the partnership, making it the company it was today.

The door finally opened, and Mark entered. "Sorry I'm late."

"It's okay." Setting his glass of water down, David opened his arms as his business partner took a seat. "So, what's up?"

"How are you doing?"

"Good. I'm going out of town this weekend, by the way, and I'm not sure of cell phone reception."

"Okay. Listen, David, we've been in business for a while now. Would you say we've had a good run?"

Furrowing his eyebrows as David detected this wasn't a conversation about the point of sale system but something more serious, he leaned toward Mark. "What do you mean? What's going on?"

"We've had an offer put on the table to buy *Carlton's*."

David responded immediately without thinking. "It's not for sale." David stood up and headed for the door, but Mark grabbed his arm.

"Wait. You don't even want to hear it?"

"No, I don't. This business is our life, Mark. We agreed to never sell."

"That was twenty years ago, David. I think we should at least talk about it. We are partners, after all."

Mark's words penetrated through his resistance. Mark was at least right about their being partners and he knew it was the right thing to do to at least talk about the offer. Letting out a defeated sigh, David turned around and returned to the chair at the table. He listened as Mark first explained how the new point of sale system was to help the image to potential buyers. Then Mark went on to explain the multi-million-dollar offer and how they'd both be set for life. It was apparent to David by the end of all the explaining that Mark hadn't thought of anyone outside of himself for months now.

"Can I ask you something?"

Mark nodded. "Absolutely."

"Did you stop and think about those people out there for one second?" David pointed to the door.

Mark shrugged. "They'll have jobs."

"Yeah, but the people coming in won't know them like we

know them. It could be pretty easy to fire some of the workforce around here."

Shaking his head, Mark leaned in and placed his arms on the table. "Are you telling me we have an over-bloated workforce here?"

"No, it's a skeleton crew, but if new people come in, they might not understand everything. In fact, they can't understand it the way we can and do! Listen, I think there is a lot more at stake and it's not just all money and glitter here. That's all I'm saying."

"It's a lot of money, David. Go home and think about it while you're on vacation this weekend. Talk to the Mrs. and really think about it. That amount of money could change your life."

"My life is fine."

"Really? You enjoy riding the shoulders of these managers and keeping tabs on everything so it goes smoothly? Sure, it's fun around here, but a lot of it is babysitting that neither of us need to do. We can be free if we take this offer." Mark pushed up the sleeve of his jacket and looked at his watch. Then, he stood up. "Think about it, David."

Mark exited the board room, shutting the door quietly behind him. David leaned back in the swivel chair and rested his hands behind his head. David didn't like this at all. He wouldn't give up the one thing that he built from the ground up to a success. *Carlton's* wasn't just a place he worked. It was his entire life.

CHAPTER 5

SATURDAY MORNING'S AIR WAS FILLED with excitement for Cindy as she made the final preparations for the trip. She had spent the last few days thanking God in prayer constantly for a chance to make things right in her marriage. There was a thread of hope illuminated now in her life, and she could barely contain her soul's joy. Cindy could sense it in David too. He had come home for dinner the last few nights and made more of an effort to communicate with her leading up to the day of the retreat. *Could this have been God's plan all along?* she gleefully thought as she placed the last piece of clothing into the suitcase.

Cindy sprayed herself with a mist of perfume before slipping it into the front pocket of the suitcase, then zipped it all up tight. David entered the bedroom.

"The car is warmed up. You ready?"

"Yes." Cindy smiled and went to reach for the suitcase, but David stopped her and took it into his hand. This weekend away was already a good thing for the two of them and it hadn't even begun yet. She followed behind David as he journeyed out to the car in the driveway.

They arrived at *The Inn At The Lake* at ten o'clock that morning. Pulling into the driveway, David slowed the car as they came beneath the shade of towering pine trees, finally stopping as he parked behind a car already in the driveway. Cindy looked at David and noticed his fingers trembling as he pulled the key from the ignition. Reaching a hand over to his arm, she gently touched him.

"It's going to be okay. They're all believers like us."

He nodded. "Let's do this."

As he opened the car door and got out, Cindy was taken aback by his comment. *Let's do this.* It was if this was some sort of task for him to complete. It unnerved her to hear him speak that way about the retreat. It reminded her too much of the old David she knew merely days ago. Her anxiety began to rise within her, but she managed to brush it off. Cindy kept in her sights the hope she had for the weekend. She joined David's side as he unloaded the suitcase in the back of the car and his backpack he brought for hiking. Together, hand in hand, they walked up the driveway toward the inn. It wasn't long before Cindy caught sight of the lake not far beyond the inn. It was just like Olivia had told her—beautiful. She turned to David.

"Isn't the lake pretty?"

"Yeah, it's nice."

Displeased again, this time with his 'nice' comment, she shook her head. "It's breath-taking, David! The way the sun is reflecting off the surface and shimmering like a thousand diamonds. And to think, God just spoke that into existence. All of it."

He didn't respond but appeared to be focused on getting to the front door. It reminded her of his offhanded comment moments ago in the car when he said, *'Let's do this.'* The anxiety came back, pushing toward the surface as she worried the last three days leading up to the retreat, and even the retreat, could possibly all be a show he's putting on. *I can't go back to the way things were in our marriage,* she thought to herself. *I can't.*

Opening the door, a woman answered.

"Hello! You must be the Carltons! I'm Serenah. We've heard so much about you! Come in and I'll show you to your room."

As Serenah showed the two of them inside, David came closer to Cindy and whispered in her ear.

"What *exactly* has she heard about us?"

Turning from the foyer to the stairs, Serenah started up the stairwell that led to an upper level floor of the inn. Pausing at the banister, Cindy shook her head and whispered a response to David. "Stop being so paranoid!"

Making their way up the stairs, Cindy could see and sense David's growing uneasiness. Even when they walked into the gorgeous room, his expression didn't shift from the disgruntled disposition he'd had since arriving in the driveway. She felt embarrassed at his ungratefulness toward Serenah.

"Serenah, this room and view are marvelous!" Cindy tried to make up for her husband's apparent lack of interest. Catching sight of the balcony off the room, Cindy was drawn to the doors that led outside. She hurried over and glanced outside. "And it has a private balcony, David!"

David nodded, no response again.

"Yes, it does!" Serenah glowed. "This is the best room we have in the inn. We drew names on the couples and you two won!"

"That is awesome." Grabbing hold of the gold-colored handles, Cindy opened the doors and stepped out onto the balcony. Turning to David, who was setting the suitcase down on the bed, she beckoned to him. "Come see this, David."

David walked over, Serenah close behind.

Cindy's heart was fluttering and her emotions at an all-time high as she turned to David. Finally, a smile broke on his face as he surveyed the lake from the vantage point of the balcony.

He turned and looked at Cindy. "This is cool."

Cindy wrapped her arms around his torso and nodded as she pressed her cheek against his chest.

"I'll catch up with you two in a bit. We'll be down in the living room when you're settled."

Releasing from her hold of David, Cindy turned to Serenah. "Thank you so much!"

"Yes, thank you," David added.

"You're welcome. See you two in a little while."

After taking in the view outside a little while longer, Cindy and David checked out the rest of the room. Arriving at the jacuzzi in the room, Cindy envisioned a lovely end to the evening taking place in that jacuzzi with David. That would be sure to re-ignite the lost flame. He must've been thinking the same thing, she thought, as he turned to her and asked, "Think we can both fit in here?"

"I do." Kissing his cheek, she wove her fingers between his. She was glad to see that David had relaxed a measure and appeared comfortable with being at the inn now. "Come on, let's go join the others downstairs."

As they traveled down the stairs and her hand was in his, Cindy's heart warmed as she felt closer to her husband than she had in years. As they entered the living room, the other couples stood up from the couches and greeted Cindy and David.

Rising to their feet, Olivia and Tyler introduced themselves first to David and shook hands.

"This is the couple who bought the painting last month," Cindy pointed out.

"The waterfall scene?" David inquired, surprising Cindy. She didn't know he had a clue about which paintings made it to the gallery.

"No." Tyler shook his head. "It was actually the painting of a raven with its wings spread out. Blues, purples and greens. Truly a beautiful and unique painting."

"Oh, yes, I remember that one now. My wife is quite talented with a paintbrush, isn't she?"

Tyler nodded, then turned to the other couple as they stood beside himself and Olivia. "This is my brother Jonathan and his wife, Kylie."

Cindy and David greeted them with handshakes. Then everyone took their seats as Serenah started talking about the plan for the weekend. She handed out small printouts that detailed the sessions that would be taking place. Saturday's focus was on husbands and wives apart from one another, and then in the evening after dinner, it would be couples' time in a group setting. Cindy glanced over at David to see how he was taking it all in, and she was delighted to see him engaged and interested.

"Today while we ladies will be working on crafts, the boys will take a row boat to the other side of the lake and hike most of the day, stopping for lunch along the way."

Just then, a door on the far wall from behind the couch opened and everyone turned their heads to see who it was.

"And that's my hubby, Charlie, coming in from the main level's deck."

He laughed and raised a hand as he kicked off his boots and walked over to the group. "Sorry about that. I had to make sure the boat's patch was holding before I trusted all of us guys to make it across."

"Good!" Tyler commented. "I don't want to sink out in the middle of the lake."

Everyone laughed. Then Olivia, with her gaze on Serenah, said, "I thought there were two other couples coming?"

"There were," Serenah replied, stopping short. "But some things came up with them and instead of filling the spots, we left them empty. This smaller group will give us a chance to focus even more on the couples in attendance."

Charlie nodded and then held out his arms. "God knew those couples would not be able to make it. I trust He is in control and we are going to see God show up in a big way through this time together as brothers and sisters in Christ. Let's pray and then we'll get the day started."

Everyone bowed their heads.

"Lord, we come to You today as followers of You and we ask You to open our hearts and minds to the wisdom and knowledge that comes from You alone. Let the Scriptures we study feed our souls with Your truth. Let our time together in fellowship with one another be unforgettable. Let us speak candidly about our lives, about our faith, and about our struggles. You are the giver of life and it's only through You that our marriages stand a chance in today's fallen world. Let us speak and do all things in Your name and in love. Amen."

CRAFT TIME CONSISTED of knitting scarves for the upcoming winter and light conversation between all the ladies about life, marriage, and children. Cindy shared the fact that she was going to be a grandmother once again and there were congratulations all around the table. As they finished up their craft just before breaking for lunch, conversation turned serious for Olivia.

"You know, I was eager to marry Tyler last summer and even happy about it, but I can't help but get worried every time we have a disagreement. I don't want to upset him and then risk his regretting his choice in me."

Everyone agreed, Cindy most of all, but she was more inwardly concerned about it than she was vocally.

Serenah must've sensed it because in the very next moment, she turned to Cindy. "You have any insight for a newlywed like Olivia? You've been married the longest here, I believe."

Cindy laughed out of nervousness more than anything. Then she shrugged. "What can I say? Marriage is hard, and I've made my fair share of mistakes. Honestly, I'm to the point in my marriage where I don't mind disagreeing and arguments. Arguments indicate communication. In my experience, what's scary is when you stop arguing and there's just silence."

"Mmm. Good point." Serenah turned to Olivia. "Arguments are healthy and to be expected in marriage. In my opinion, when character assassination enters the conversation from either side, you've got to take a step back. Ripping each other apart is no way to solve *any* issue, and it's not okay. God tells us in the Bible to let our words build each other up (Ephesians 4:29) and to focus on the good in life (Philippians 4:8). When we focus on the bad and on the flaws of one another, we give the enemy a foothold in our lives."

Kylie jumped in. "God knows Jonathan and I have had our share of disagreements in our marriage. My husband had to learn to love all over again after he lost his wife Marie, and it took a while for me to become really comfortable with certain facts about him. For instance, there's a part of Jonathan that will always love another woman, his first wife, and through the power of God, I've been able to be okay with that. The worst thing in the world we can do is get into a frame of mind that *we* are the ones who can fix someone to be how we want them. Only

God can do that, and oftentimes, we are the ones who need fixing."

Guilt weighed on Cindy's heart as she knew some of her comments, the vile ones especially, were her attempts at fixing David and the marriage.

"I love that last part you said." Serenah opened her arms, palms up, on the table. "Only God can fix the brokenness. We have to rely on God and trust in *Him* alone to fix, mend, and repair the hurts in this life we encounter. When we allow Him to be God in our lives, we can see big changes or change in a big way."

After putting away their knitting needles and yarn, Serenah served each of the ladies a pita sandwich and a small pile of chips. The temperature outside had climbed up to mid-sixties, and with a light jacket on, Cindy went outside to eat with the ladies on the main-level deck that faced the lake.

"This inn is so beautiful." Cindy's eyes drank in the view of the pristine lake view once again. "I can't get over it. It must be wonderful to live here."

Cindy then took her first bite of the pita sandwich.

Serenah nodded, looking at the water. "God's glory is painted all over this place out here. It took time to truly see it though." Her eyes fell to the side portion of the deck and toward a patch of the inn's property that was covered in a thick patch of trees. She appeared to be lost in a thought hidden away in her mind. Then she turned to the ladies. "I had a daughter before Emma, but I lost her in pregnancy. I built a memorial over in those trees there."

Everyone turned to see where she was pointing. A gasp sounded from the ladies.

"My point in telling you this is the fact that my life is a testimony of God's grace and goodness. I was destroyed by losing my unborn child, but God healed me. Fixed me. In the end, He blessed me with a beautiful baby girl. Emma. Sure, it still hurts to think about losing that child all those years ago, but it's okay now. That precious soul didn't have to face the difficulties that this life has to offer. Instead, that baby is in Heaven with Jesus. Some might say we don't deserve some of the tragedies we face in life, but the reality is we don't deserve anything good. The only true injustice to a 'good person' was when Jesus was nailed to a cross, and He did it willingly."

Cindy felt inspired by the way Serenah spoke about her faith. It encouraged her to know others suffered too, but in their own ways, and that there was hope for everyone.

CHAPTER 6

THE JOURNEY FOR THE MEN'S hike took them across Diamond Lake, through a forest, and up a relatively steep mountain. When they broke for lunch at noon, David was already worn out. Taking a deep drink from his canteen, he wiped his mouth on his sleeve and peered across the treetops and down toward the lake.

"It's all downhill from here." Tyler patted David's shoulder as he smiled and joined his gaze across the scenery.

David let out a laugh. "That's a good thing. I don't know how much more I could take!"

Tyler raised his eyebrows and nodded. "It's a good deal of exercise, making it up here." As Tyler spoke, David caught a glimpse of Charlie pulling out a Bible from his backpack and opening it.

He hadn't seen much of a Bible outside of Sunday morning for a long time. He still loved the Lord and thought of Him often, even prayed on occasion, but Bible reading and his devotional time overall had fallen to the wayside. It started with missing a few days here and there, and then before he knew it, it was weeks, then months, and eventually, it led to years. There was no malice or ill will in his choices. Other things in life just got in the way. Other things became more important. After Tyler went to speak with his brother Jonathan a few feet away, David got up and went over to Charlie.

"Whatcha you reading?" David slid his backpack off his shoulders and unzipped the front pocket, placing his canteen back inside.

"1 Peter 2." Charlie called for Jonathan and Tyler to join them. As they all formed a circle around Charlie, everyone took a seat. "Let's open in a word of prayer and then we'll read some of God's Word. Lord, we come to You today as men. Men who want to do right by You, God. Men who seek to honor You in all that we do, all that we say, and all that we are. We are husbands, we are fathers, but first, we are followers of Jesus. You are the Lord of not only our actions in everyday life, but the Lord over our inner men. The character and heart are what You seek after, and we want to give it all to You. We pray You shape us, mold us, and make us into men of courage and strength in a dying and fallen world. We ask You to bless the time in Your Word today and open our hearts and minds to Your truths. Amen."

All the men, in sync, said, 'Amen.'

"As I mentioned in our prayer a moment earlier, we are living in a fallen world. As men, we are leaders over our homes. Even if our children are grown and out of the house." His eyes connected with David's before continuing. "Let's read 1 Peter 2:11-12."

Dear friends, I urge you, as foreigners and exiles, to abstain from sinful desires, which wage war against your soul.

Live such good lives among the pagans that, though they accuse you of doing wrong, they may see your good deeds and glorify God on the day he visits us.

1 Peter 2:11-12

"AS CHRISTIANS, we are foreigners in this world. Our home isn't here. Our home is in Heaven." Charlie stood up and pointed back toward the way they had hiked. "While we can see God's glorious hand all over creation, like we do right at this vantage point, what we see in our daily lives is a world that is dying. Men, our residency is not this place, but we must be fighting day in and day out against the sinful desires of our flesh. If you think for a second you're not in a fight, you're being deceived. When I ask what the devil looks like, what honestly comes to your minds, brothers?"

Jonathan piped up. "Red-skinned evil dude with a pitchfork."

Charlie nodded. "That's right." He started to shake his head. "But that's a lie. The devil is not some scary demonic-looking cartoon character. The devil is attractive, the devil is seductive to our sinful flesh. Our heart in this fallen state holds within it sinful desires. Whether it's the cute new receptionist at work or the delicious piece of low-hanging fruit from the forbidden tree in the garden of Eden. The enemy wants to trip us up and cause us to fall, to stumble, to doubt God's plan, to doubt God Himself. 1 Peter 2:11 says, 'abstain from sinful desires, which wage war against your soul.' The question this presents is this. How do we abstain? I'll tell you. We stay in our Bibles." Patting his open Bible, he continued. "The Bible is our refuge, and we have to soak up the words of God daily into our hearts so there isn't any room for the devil, isn't any room for our selfishness. We must renew our minds daily. Right now in this world, Satan's hand is so strong, men. Through the Internet, he is pushing pornography, through Hollywood in movies and on TV, he is pushing fornication, and with our young kids, he is pushing agendas that lead to confusion, lies, and chaos. *'Be whatever gender you feel you are.'* But guess what, guys? We have the Truth right here in God's Word. The Bible is our greatest weapon against the battles we face every single day, no matter what it is. Ephesians 6:12 tells us, 'For our struggle is not against flesh and blood, but against the rulers, against the authorities, against the powers of this dark world and against the spiritual forces of evil in the heavenly realms.' This means we have to be on guard. As men, as leaders, as followers of Jesus, we have to be filled with God's truth and that means being in His Word."

Charlie paused, then his voice lowered.

"As men, we have to lead first by example in our homes, in our daily lives. The Scripture here in 1 Peter goes on to tell us to live such good lives that nobody can accuse us of wrong-doing. That's a heavy responsibility, and it's impossible without God on our side. Men, our children look up to us whether they still live in the home or have gone on to make their own families. Our wives are looking at us too! We are accountable."

As Charlie continued talking, David's heart felt an increasing heaviness. Conviction of his actions pelted against his whole being. He knew things needed to change before he came to the retreat, but he was starting to understand that the change was with him. After Charlie finished speaking, it was time to make the trek back down the mountain. David pulled Charlie aside to speak with him privately away from the other men.

"Hey. That mini-sermon was hard for me to hear, but in a good way. I really want a change to happen in my marriage. I just don't know how to do it."

"Okay. Listen, only God can bring real and lasting change. Can I pray with you, David? Right now?"

"Yes, I'd love that."

"Okay." Placing a hand on David's shoulder, Charlie led the two of them in a prayer. "God, this weekend is about You coming into our lives, hearts, and marriages in a *big* way. David needs Your help. I need Your help. We all need Your help. I pray a special prayer on David that you lead him in the way he should go and help him be the man of God You desire. Amen."

As they lifted their eyes from prayer, David thanked him.

"You're welcome. I don't know the details of what's going on in your marriage and I don't need to. All I know is when our priorities get tangled and we take our eyes off Jesus, that's when things become difficult. Focus on God, Brother."

"You're right. Thank you."

After the prayer with Charlie, David began to feel some of the heaviness in his heart loosen. Yanking on the straps of his backpack, David adjusted it slightly and fell into step with the guys on their way down the mountain. He still felt a little winded from the initial journey and the sermon, but he had hopes of a changed future ahead for him and Cindy.

AS THEY CROSSED the lake by boat, David leaned a hand over the edge of the boat and let his fingertips glide atop the chilly water. He'd had some worry over the trip to the inn with Cindy, but he was more hopeful than ever that it was going to turn out to be the best decision he had ever made. After exiting the boat at the dock, the men joined the ladies in the inn, then everybody retreated to their rooms to take some alone time with their wives. As David told Cindy about the sermon he heard atop the mountain, he could see Cindy's face radiating joy.

"I love seeing you like this, David. It's like a light finally came on in your head."

He didn't like her comment. David stopped talking and furrowed his brows.

"What?"

He didn't respond but instead walked across the room and over to the French doors that led out to their private balcony. Opening them, he walked out and took a deep breath of air into his lungs. *Lord, give me strength not to battle with her.* He didn't want to fight, not after such a pleasant day with the men. Soon, Cindy joined him out on the balcony and rested a hand on his back.

"David, what's wrong? Talk to me."

"You want to talk." He shook his head as a sardonic laugh escaped his lips. "That's funny, coming from you!"

He regretted his words immediately after they had slipped from his mouth. Though he had a wonderful hike with the men, the hurt from the affair was still present in his heart. It lurked in the shadows of his mind and heart, just waiting to be pulled out and put on display, an old wound that he refused to let heal. She acted like he had all the issues and mistakes when it was her fault that started it all. His mind went into blame mode. *If she had been willing to talk then, maybe he could've helped steer her in a different direction and the affair wouldn't have happened.* Cindy never came to him in those days. Instead, she went out and found someone else to talk to instead of him, someone else she thought could satisfy her needs the way he hadn't. David's heart ached deeply in that moment on the balcony and it felt as if his soul was tearing. "I'm sorry, I shouldn't have said that."

"What did you mean by that comment, David?"

He shook his head, raising his hands. "No, just drop it. Please?"

"No, tell me." David resisted, but then she grabbed his arm, insisting that he speak.

"Jeremy!" He blurted out the name of her art teacher she'd had the affair with from the community college.

The name alone made Cindy stop and take a step back. David could see something within her move, and it hurt him on the deepest level to see her still affected by the man's name.

"That was so long ago, David. Why can't you let this go?"

"Because in my head and heart, it feels like yesterday. Don't you get it? I don't know how to forget about it, how to stop it from torturing me! It's there when I wake up, it's there when I pillow my head at night. It eats at my soul every moment of every day."

Her cheeks were moist with tears now, and David's heart ached deeply to see her in pain, pain that he had put there. He had to take his shovel out every chance he got and dig it all up again for her, making her live through the painful mistake all over again. He hated himself for mentioning it.

She was quiet, not responding with anything other than her tears.

David traded his heartache for anger in the moment and became upset. He flung a hand in the air as he turned and went inside from the balcony. Traveling through the room, he went into the bathroom and shut the door behind him, locking it. Peering into the mirror, he smoothed his hands over his face. *What do You want me to do, God? Just show me.*

Turning the faucet on, he turned it to cold. He splashed the chilled water into his eyes and across his face. The coolness settled his nerves. After toweling his face with a hand towel, he exited the bathroom to find Cindy lying on her side on the bed, her knees drawn up into her chest in the fetal position.

David's heart ached. Walking over to the bed, he sat down beside her and gently placed a hand on her side.

"You ready to go down?"

She didn't look at him at all. In a damp and defeated tone, she spoke gently. "What's the point?"

He moved his hand from her side to her shoulder, then smoothed the side of his thumb softly against her shirt. "Cindy, I know this is hard and I'm sorry for digging up the past like that yet again. I know the way I've been acting for a long time isn't right, but if we're going to fix what's wrong, we have to keep moving forward."

Sitting up, she wiped her reddened eyes. Sniffling, she blinked her eyes, appearing to ward off the tears.

"David." Cindy said his name but paused for a moment before continuing. "You can't throw the past in my face over and over again and expect us to ever heal or fix what's wrong."

"I know." David's head hung in shame for a moment, then he moved both his hands to grasp hold of hers. Then, he peered into her eyes. "I can't promise you it'll be all sunshine and rainbows from this point on in our marriage. I don't know how dark the night will get before we start heading toward the light of the sunrise. But I do know this. I want us."

Smiling through a frown, she wiped her tears away once more. "I love you, David."

In that moment, David not only heard his wife say the words, but he felt them too. His heart radiated with warmth from her love and he smiled.

"I love you too." Leaning toward her, David kissed her lips softly, then hugged her. He took her by the hand a moment later and they traveled downstairs and rejoined the others.

AFTER DINNER LATER THAT EVENING, all the couples followed

Serenah out to the main level deck for a special surprise. Charlie had already slipped away shortly after dinner without a word about what he was doing. It wasn't long after Cindy and David had taken their seats beside each other on two patio chairs that a loud boom from the lake sounded, startling everyone. Then the sky lit up with an explosion of color. Fireworks. David peered across the lake and spotted a shadowy figure sitting in a canoe out on the water. *Charlie,* he thought with a smile. He scooted closer to Cindy and placed his arm around her shoulders. Watching the variety of colors light up the starry sky reminded him of the first time he and Cindy had officially met. It was so long ago, but a night he'd never forget.

A moment passed, and Cindy leaned into his ear. "The Ferris wheel."

His heart warmed at realization that she had been thinking of the same night.

CHAPTER 7

September 2, 1991

WALKING WITH HER GROUP OF College-age girlfriends through the gates of the county fair, Cindy looked forward to a night she'd never forget. Her wealthy friends Alisha and Hillary had bought them all wristbands to go on all the carnival rides and even had spending money for treats. It wasn't just going to be a girls' night out. There was a group of guys from their college that would be meeting up with them, including James Peterson, the guy Cindy had been crushing on since September when she started at Eastern Washington University. He was Mister Popular around campus and the star quarterback for the football team. Every girl wanted him, including herself.

When the boys finally met up with them, two hours past the six o'clock time they all had agreed on, they took the girls to a spot under the bleachers of the arena. Tommy, one of the guys, slid off his backpack and opened it up to reveal a glass bottle of an amber liquid. Immediately, Cindy took a step back, knowing it was alcohol.

"What's wrong, Cindy? We're just going to have a little

fun," Her friend Elise was egging her on. "It's just something to loosen us up to have a fun time tonight."

"Yeah, don't be a prude," James said, then handed her a red plastic cup. She sat down on the concrete, and everyone else did too. Swirling the amber liquid around in the bottom of the cup, she debated what to do. On one hand, she knew it wasn't right by everything she learned growing up at home, but on the other hand, James Peterson and the others were looking at her.

In an instant, she made her decision and gulped it down. Coughing as she choked the substance down, she shook her head and pushed the cup away from her.

"That is foul tasting!"

The others laughed. Then Elise handed her a can of soda. "Drink that. It'll get rid of the taste."

As she took a swig of the soda, the taste of the alcohol washed out from her mouth. The red cup went around the circle of young adults, being refilled several times over the next few minutes. Cindy didn't feel the effects, so she agreed to another drink from the cup as long as she could have Elise's soda nearby to wash the taste away again. In her mind, she had already taken a taste, so she might as well see what it felt like. A few minutes passed, and the cup went back into Tommy's backpack and everyone stood up to leave. Cindy was disappointed with the lack of results as she lingered a while longer in the sitting position. *What's wrong with me?* She wondered. *Did God make me immune to alcohol?*

"Come on. Let's go on the rides." Elise stuck a hand out to help her up.

"I just didn't feel anything from it. Seems like it's over-hyped." Grabbing hold her friend's hand, Cindy rose to her feet. As her feet pressed against the flatness of the concrete, her head took a spin. "Whoa."

"Hitting you now?" Elise laughed.

Nausea set in a moment later, but Cindy grabbed hold of the bleacher seats near her and the icky feeling passed a moment later. "Little bit."

Elise gently brought a hand to Cindy's back. "You okay?"

As her gaze fixed ahead, she saw James and the other guys talking near the exit toward the fair. "James is really here. That's so cool."

Laughing, Elise said, "Yep, and he's waiting. Let's go."

As the two of them caught up with the guys and the three other girls, they fell into stride together as a group and ventured through the fairgrounds. The fair that year had a record turnout due to the biker convention falling on the same week, and it made for a densely populated crowd. Their entire group filed into the long line for the roller coaster and Cindy had another wave of nausea rise within her. Covering her mouth as she worried she might become ill on James, who was only a few feet from her, she turned away from the line she was in and looked out, fixating her eyes on a carnival game of darts.

Elise leaned into her ear. "I can save your spot if you need to use the restroom."

Another wave hit before she could say she was fine and Cindy nodded. "I think that might be best. I'll be back."

Maneuvering between the line of people, she spotted a restroom a few feet from where she was and headed for it. The gag reflex tickled in her throat and she knew she wasn't going to make it if she didn't run, so she took off in a sprint. Entering the bathroom, she spotted an open stall and went for it quickly. As the toilet fell into her view, she expelled the contents of her stomach. It came so violently she fell to her knees. The skin of her knees rested on damp pieces of toilet paper and other refuse she didn't want to know about.

Wiping her mouth as she thought she had finished, she felt another wave come on and she draped her head back over the foul toilet. *Stupid girl,* she thought to herself. Then between pauses, she prayed and asked for forgiveness, pleading with God that she'd never drink again. How could she have been so dumb to fall into peer pressure? All for a boy? *Hope he is worth it,* she scolded herself as she began another round of the emptying of her stomach. By the time the nausea had left her, she knew they had most likely already gone on the ride and had moved on elsewhere. Wiping her mouth and her knees off, she washed her face, fixed her makeup, and returned to the fairgrounds.

Cindy checked the roller coaster and saw they were gone. She started to stroll the fairgrounds alone. Taking in the scenes, she saw families, and it made her think of her own back in Georgia. She missed her mother and father and looked forward more than ever to her first trip back home in a couple of months for winter break. With her nausea absent now along with her dinner from earlier in the night, her stomach grumbled as she entered the food court area of the fair. She grabbed a bowl of Teriyaki chicken and rice and continued the hunt for her friends while she ate.

As she walked by the swing ride, she finally spotted someone familiar, but it was only Elise and James. As she walked toward them, she was about to call out to her friend Elise when James leaned in and kissed her so-called friend.

She stopped.

Pitching the remainder of her food into the garbage can nearby, she walked furiously through the crowd. Glancing upward, she saw the Ferris wheel and it reminded her of a distinct memory she had with her father when she was a little girl. He was fearful of heights, but after she had discovered the painful realization of the carnival games' trickery, he was moved with compassion and offered to take her on the Ferris wheel. While he grabbed hold of whatever he could get his hands on in the ride and sang, "Jesus loves me," she was overwhelmed by his unyielding love. She needed that love right about now and she longed for it. She went straight for the Ferris wheel, still alone.

She waited in line, then when she arrived at the platform to board the ride, the man shook his head and pointed to the sign. "Need two."

"But I'm an adult. I'll be fine."

He shook his head.

Her eyes moistened, and her gaze shifted up at the Ferris wheel as her hopes of recapturing a precious moment from her simpler days as a child vanished. Then she turned her eyes back on the man. "Please?"

"Two."

A man's voice sounded from behind her in the line. "I'll go with you."

She turned to see who it was, and it was someone familiar, but she couldn't place his face in her mind. Tilting her head, she was befuddled.

"That is, if it's okay with you." His warm brown eyes connected with her soul and she felt a spark within her ignite at that very moment.

"That's fine, I guess." She shrugged a shoulder and acted like he hadn't just made her wish come true. She didn't want to seem too happy, too desperate. As they climbed aboard and then started up to the heights of the sky, the sounds of the fair became quiet, fading into the distance. It was peaceful as they climbed into the air, and she closed her eyes, recalling her father and that night so long ago.

"I'm David. What's your name?"

She blinked her eyes open and turned to him. "Cindy."

"Cindy, like Cindy Lou Who."

She laughed. "Yes, if you're into Dr. Seuss. By the way, thank you. I really needed this."

"You needed a Ferris wheel ride?"

"Yes." Cindy hesitated to continue with the stranger.

"You don't remember me. Do you?"

"From where?"

"Freshman orientation. I was the guy who held open the door for you."

She laughed as she shook her head. "I'm afraid I don't."

"Well . . . I remember you."

Her heart warmed at hearing his words. She had felt invisible much of her time at college thus far. Her 'friends' she had come with were just girls from the dorm she had met a week ago. And while her so-called friends had seemed to have forgotten her in the bathroom after they had poisoned her, this kind-hearted stranger had not only ridden with her on the ride but remembered her. Cindy scooted closer to him in the cart and he brought his arm up behind her. Cindy had found a slice of comfort that night and she knew he was someone special.

CHAPTER 8

DAVID ROSE EARLY THE FOLLOWING day, Sunday, at the inn. It was quite early, five o'clock, to be precise. After brewing a pot of coffee, he took a cup with him along with his Bible that Cindy had packed in their suitcase and walked into the living room. Turning the lamp on at the end table beside the couch, he settled into a comfortable spot on the couch. He let out a large sigh as he cracked open the Bible and randomly turned to the book of James. He started reading.

A half hour had passed in the silence before he heard low voices coming from somewhere down the stairs off the foyer. He stole a glance toward the stairwell, curious to know who else was awake. Emerging moments later was Tyler. David shot him a friendly smile, then grabbed his cup of coffee from the coffee table and took a drink. Tyler went into the kitchen, returning moments later with his own mug of coffee. Tyler sat down beside him on the couch.

They spoke in low voices.

"Hey, man. Getting some time in with the Lord?"

"Yes. I'll be honest, this kind of thing hasn't really

happened much in a long time. What's funny is how natural and right it feels to my soul to be reading the Bible. I feel disappointed in myself with how I've been living so far."

"I think our flesh plays tricks on us to make us think negatively about some things, like church and Bible reading. I remember a time in my life where going to church was the biggest hassle! These trivial things in our life get in the way of a relationship with God and it's so sad. Thankfully, God forgives us. Thank God for His grace and mercy being new each day."

"Amen to that." David shifted his position on his couch to face Tyler more directly. "How long have you been married to Olivia?"

"Just over a year. Why do you ask?"

"I saw you two at dinner last night. The way you were all kissy and lovey-dovey made me think it was rather new. The honeymoon stage is wonderful."

Tyler laughed, his cheeks reddening. "Yeah. We're pretty into each other."

"Why'd you come to a marriage retreat then?"

He shrugged. "Same as my brother, I think. We just want to make sure we're keeping on top of our marriages. Proactive instead of reactive. You know? I don't think we have issues going on in either of our marriages, but I know for me, I'm always interested in learning how I can do better by my wife. I'm called to love my wife the way Christ loves His church, and I know I'm not doing that a hundred percent. There is *always* room for improvement."

"That's really wise of you." David glanced away, thinking about how that kind of mindset could benefit his own marriage to Cindy. Life had been so much easier and clearer when they were younger. He'd meet her at her dorm and bring a nice box of chocolates or a flower and she was happy as a clam. There were no work demands, no children pulling for their attention. It was just two crazy kids in love. Simple.

Tyler broke the silence a few moments later. "You know, I lost a close friend to me a while back. His name was Chip. You remind me a lot of him, David."

"Oh, yeah?"

"Yes. He loved his wife like crazy all the years she was alive."

"You see that in me?"

"Of course. I saw you pull that chair out for Cindy last night at dinner. Even after a long time of being married, you do little things like that? That is awesome. I like that. I hope to be like that. I also noticed how long your eyes lingered on her when she got up to take her dinner plate into the kitchen. How long have you been married?"

"Twenty-six years." David's heart smiled, but he was quickly saddened knowing that he hadn't been doing those little kind things for her in recent years. "Honestly, those little things are just recently returning, as of a few days ago. I've made a lot of mistakes. It is nice to hear someone on the outside seeing my love for her. Tyler, me and that woman have been through a lot over the years and it's been hard. Life has a way of wearing a person down sometimes, and I think that's what happened to me."

"Well, what's important is you're doing it again. And you're here. Both good things. Thing about life wearing us down is that this world isn't our true home, like Charlie was saying yesterday on the hike. If we get too caught up in it, we can be dragged away. You know?"

Tyler's words touched his soul and convicted David in that moment of his sin. The cares of this world had dragged him away. "That's the truth."

"I know it's a constant struggle in my own heart." Touching his chest, Tyler continued. "I have to yield to Jesus every single day and keep a close rein on my thoughts especially, bringing every thought under submission of Christ. I notice this world has a lot of distractions that can pull us away."

"It's true. We wear multiple hats. I'm a dad, a husband, and a boss. It seems like there's *always* something or someone there that needs my attention."

"And yet God says I want it all." Tyler smiled. "He really is a jealous God, isn't He? But I mean, that's a good thing. It's not like a jealous spouse. God is perfect. He wants our hearts on Him because He knows that is what we actually need!"

Nodding slowly as David dipped his head with a measure of shame, he responded to Tyler. "And even after forty-eight years on this earth, I'm still figuring that out."

Tyler chuckled lightly, patting David's back. "Same here, Brother. Same here."

A COUPLE OF HOURS LATER, everyone was finally awake, and Charlie made breakfast. As everybody sat at the tables in the dining area, discussing the fireworks from last night and how amazing the lake view out their windows was to wake up to, Charlie came over with stacks of French toast piled onto plates. Serenah let out a laugh.

"Dear! You didn't need to make *that* much food! You made enough to feed a small army."

Charlie laughed as he set the plates of French toast down on two separate tables that had been pushed together to accommodate everyone.

"Nobody is going hungry on my watch! Just another couple of minutes and the sausage links will be done."

"This is amazing, Charlie. Thank you!" Jonathan stuck his fork into three pieces and brought them down onto his plate. "Do you have peanut butter?"

Serenah tilted her head. "What? Peanut butter?"

"Yes, it's in the pantry. Come grab it," Charlie responded from inside the kitchen.

"Yes. French toast is *amazing* with peanut butter." Jonathan rose from his seat and walked over to the kitchen.

Everyone agreed that it was strange, but Kylie spoke up.

"I had an Uncle Ben who did it all the time growing up."

"Does he do it with pancakes too?" Serenah inquired of Kylie, but she shook her head.

"Only French toast," Jonathan said as he returned with a butter knife full of peanut butter. He slathered it on, getting a cringe from Cindy as he did.

"What's the plan today? Church?" David asked, his words focused toward Serenah.

"We have a guest speaker filling in for Charlie today at the church so we could be here. Do you still have your handout I gave you?"

"Oh, yeah." David recalled its whereabouts. "But that's in the back pocket of my jeans upstairs in the room."

"Okay, well this morning, Charlie will preach from Corinthians and then we will work on discovering each other's love language. Today's going to be a blessing for each one of us. I just know it!"

After breakfast and the sermon from Charlie, each couple broke away into a private area to work on discovering each other's love language. Cindy and David took to a small lovely table in the lower-level living room to work on their worksheet. As David learned about his wife's love language being words of affirmation, he was overwhelmed with a sense of guilt.

He let out a long sigh.

"What's wrong?" Cindy leaned across the table, concern evident in her eyes.

Shrugging, David shook his head. "We've been married

for a long time and I just now figured out your love language is words of affirmation?" He laughed lightly, embarrassed by the fact that he didn't know his wife as well as he thought he did. "I had no idea and I'm truly sorry for that. You're an amazing woman and I love you."

She smiled, tilting her head. "For a lot of years, you spoke my love language. It wasn't until . . ."

Her hesitation caused him concern. David leaned in over the table. "Until what?"

"I don't want to blame you for my mistakes, David."

"Then don't. I just want to know when it stopped. I want to know when you thought I stopped loving you."

"Okay." She paused, glancing up at the ceiling for a moment as if she were fishing memories from some back corner pond in her mind. "Remember when you and Mark got that big client, Alvin's Custard? About ten years ago?"

A smile broke across his face, remembering when *Carlton's* finally went from red to black financially. "Do I ever! It was twelve years ago. We finally started making real money at *Carlton's* and I was able to pay off all our debt that same year! Then we were able to buy the land we live on and build our dream house!"

"Yeah, great year financially . . ." Again, she hesitated, but David pleaded for her to continue with the look in his eyes. "But you were gone a lot more. When you did get home, you'd sit in front of the television and zone out or argue with contractors about the house."

His defense walls went up and he snapped. "I was working a lot to provide for our family! We were getting everything we finally deserved that year because of my hard work!"

Cindy just looked at him, not saying anything but really looking at him. His heart caught up with his mouth and he realized his error. "I shouldn't justify myself. I asked, and I do want to hear."

"Thank you. Those days were the start of something bad within me."

He couldn't believe what he was hearing. It hurt him deeply to know that when things started getting good with his business is when things started going south for his wife. As she continued to detail out his mistakes and shortcomings in their marriage in the last decade, it became too much for David's heart to bear and he stood up from the table. She stopped talking as he walked over to the French doors leading out to the deck. He looked out at the lake as a growing ache radiated inside his chest. He had blamed all the pain in his life on his wife, but he was starting to see he had a part in it all too, and that fact crushed him.

A few moments passed, then Cindy spoke from her seat at the table. "David?"

Turning to her, he raised an eyebrow as he could see her eyes glistening with tears. "Yeah?"

"I'm sorry I wasn't a better wife and able to handle it." Tears started to trickle from her eyes and down her cheeks. He realized she felt plenty of guilt on her own without his layering it on. Moved with compassion for his wife, he walked over to her, bent a knee down, and put his arms around her.

"I don't want to hold the past over you, and I promise I won't bring it up again." Reaching out, he rested his hand on the worksheet. "I'm going to do to a better job at loving you the way you need to be loved, Cindy. I promise."

Moving her arms, she wrapped them around David and his heart radiated with a pulsating joy. As David held his wife close to himself, he felt he was right where God wanted him. Glancing up at the ceiling, David thanked God for his wife and the weekend trip to the inn.

CHAPTER 9

ARRIVING HOME THAT EVENING, THE house was the same, but the air felt different to Cindy. She could sense the love alive again between her and David. Joy filled her heart as she unpacked their suitcase and loaded the washer with the dirty clothes from their trip. Could a couple of brief days really have such a profound impact on their marriage? She wasn't sure of the answer, but all signs were pointing to a resounding 'yes.' As she came out of the laundry room and passed through the hallway toward the bedroom, she could hear David on the phone just down the hallway in the kitchen.

She wondered who he was talking to as she went into the bedroom and took the empty suitcase to the closet. As she slid it back behind her dresses in the closet, David came into the room.

"Hey, that was Tyler."

Lifting an eyebrow as she stood upright and turned to him, she was surprised to hear he had called. "I didn't know he had your number."

"We chatted for a while this morning and exchanged

contact information. He was calling to tell me about a Bible study Charlie does with him and Jonathan, and other guys come too when they can make it. Anyway, he asked if I wanted to go."

Cindy's heart leapt, and her lips curled into a smile. "Yeah?"

"I'm going to go. I don't care for the long drive out to the lake every week, but I know it'll be worth it. I'll have accountability partners, and that's exactly what I need right now in life."

I guess a couple of days is all it takes! she thought, closing the distance between her and David. "You came back a different man, David, and I mean that in the best possible way."

"Jesus let the scales fall from my eyes." Leaning in, David kissed her cheek. "You look beautiful today, by the way. I'm not sure if I told you that since we left the inn."

Laughing, she pushed her fingers through her unkempt hair. "Whatever. I'm in sweats and a baggy spaghetti-stained T-shirt."

He snickered and shook his head. "It doesn't matter. You're still beautiful to me."

Her heart smiled, and she had hope this newness in her husband would stay. "I need to call my sister back, and then I'm going to go work on my painting for a bit and then I'll make us dinner."

"Painting? Sister? I thought we could spend some time together."

"Honey, we just spent the weekend together. I need to get this painting finished, then we can do whatever you wish."

David grinned, then waved a hand through the air. "Forget dinner. Just order some Chinese food after you get done. I'm sure you're tired from being on the trip. I know I am."

Cindy nodded, soaking up her husband's newfound care for her wellbeing. "I am."

As she parted ways with David and headed down the hallway, she thought about his comment about wanting to spend time with her. *Is he trying too hard?* She wondered for a moment. *It seems like too much.* Crossing through the kitchen, she stopped at the counter where her cellphone was and dialed her sister. It went to voicemail. She shrugged it off and went to the fridge and grabbed a bottle of water, then went into the sun room. As her eyes fell onto the painting as it sat on the easel, she let her thoughts fall away in order to focus.

The painting spoke differently to her than it did last time she had visited the canvas. Instead of a painful reminder of how life used to be a long time ago, the painting gave her a stirring of rekindled love and hope. She smiled and thought of David. She once again thought about his desire to spend time with her. *Don't be alarmed by his change. Embrace it,* she told herself this time. Sitting down, she breathed in and then let it out. *It's a good thing.* She began to prepare her palette with the colors she wanted to use. Then, she picked up a brush and launched into detailing the rocks in the lake's shoreline.

AFTER DINNER, her sister Sarah from California returned her call. It turned out her husband Levi hadn't been home in over a week. She hadn't mentioned that in her text last week. Levi had done this once before, and when he finally did get home, Sarah got a beating that almost killed her. She had a concussion and four stitches in the back of her skull after her trip to the E.R. for what she told the doctors happened from 'falling down the stairs'. Sarah *always* lied for Levi. Sarah had reached out when Levi had left that time too. She'd asked if she could come live with David and Cindy, but David had insisted on it not happening. As her sister went on and on with the details about Levi on the phone this time, Cindy knew she couldn't turn her down again. She glanced at her husband. He was reclined in his chair, reading the Sunday newspaper.

"Hold on, Sis."

Covering the phone with her hand, Cindy peered over at David. Her heart hammered in her chest as she worried David might say no, just like last time. Part of her wanted to ignore David and just tell Sarah to jump on a plane and come, but she didn't dare to mess things up between her and David, especially not now.

"Hey, honey?"

Setting his paper down, he pulled off his reading glasses and looked over at her.

"Sarah needs a place to stay. Levi left again, and you remember what happened last time. What do you think?"

He grimaced for a moment but then nodded slowly. "I don't like it, but I don't want her to get hurt again. Tell her if she comes, she can't go back to him this time. She needs to really leave him for good."

Though Cindy knew she couldn't force her sister to do anything, she wasn't going to risk an argument with David. She had too much to lose. *It'll be fine,* she told herself. Returning to the call, she told her sister she could come.

"Yes! I can't believe he said I could come!" Sarah's voice carried a hope that wasn't present at the start of that phone call. Now wasn't a good time for Sarah to come, but Cindy felt she didn't have a choice if she wanted her sister safe.

"You're leaving him for good this time, Sis?" In a roundabout way, Cindy was trying to encourage her sister in the correct direction for her life. Last time this happened, Sarah only tried to lie to Cindy for a minute before revealing the truth. It turned out while he was gone, Levi had done more drugs than he could remember along with spending time and money with high-priced Los Angeles prostitutes. Cindy wept when she heard all the details Levi willingly told Sarah, a dedicated believer in Jesus Christ.

"Yes, I'm done with him for good. Jeez." Sarah let out a sigh. "Why can't people ever believe in me? Just once, it'd be nice if someone actually thought I could make a smart choice in life!"

"Well, Sis . . . you know how the saying goes, 'The past is the best indicator of the future.' "

"Yeah, my future ain't looking too good based on that logic. Got it. Well, I'm going to prove you wrong, along with everyone else."

Cindy smiled. "I love your strong-willed nature, Sarah. Keep that. You can prove everyone wrong, including those in your past, if you put your mind to it! I believe in you!"

Hearing David snicker lightly caused Cindy to glance over at him with dagger eyes. He folded the newspaper and set it down on the recliner and then went into the kitchen.

She turned her attention back to the call with Sarah. "Let me know when you're flying in and I'll pick you. Okay?"

"Sounds good. Thanks again, Cindy!"

After hanging up with Sarah, Cindy got up from the couch and went into the kitchen to find David. He was filling a glass with water.

"What were you laughing about in there?"

He shook his head, then took a deep drink of the water. Wiping his mouth a moment later, he looked at her. "Don't worry about it."

Unsatisfied with his answer, Cindy crossed the kitchen and over to him, blocking his desired walking path that led back to the living room.

David let out a sigh and opened his arms. "C'mon, this again? I don't want to talk about it."

"Well, I need you to communicate with me. I can handle it."

Rubbing his neck, he hesitated a moment longer, then gave up, letting out a sigh. "You were telling her that if she puts her mind to doing life without him, she'll do it."

"Yeah. What's so wrong with that?"

"It's cliché to say, 'If you put your mind to it, you can do anything.' And for her, especially, it's unpractical. She needs counseling, a steady job, and a dedicated routine if she wants to *move on* from this loser. You and I both know Sarah and know none of what is needed will happen."

Cindy didn't respond for a long moment. She was upset with her husband and the fact that he didn't agree that Sarah had a chance. Then, Cindy shrugged. "You know, David. If you take a person's hope away from them, what will they have left?"

"You make a good point there. I'm sorry."

Side-stepping, David continued onward to the living room. Cindy smiled, feeling as if what she had said really was heard by him, and it overjoyed her.

THE NEXT MORNING, Cindy awoke to a kiss from David on the forehead. Then he smoothed a hand over her shoulder and wished her well in the day ahead. As she heard the bedroom door shut behind him a moment later, she grinned. She felt more loved by David in the last week than she had in the last decade. Drifting to sleep once more that morning, she was able to sneak another couple of hours of shuteye before finally waking up.

Pushing the sheets and comforter off from the bed, she arose and went into the kitchen to get a cup of coffee. Seeing her nearly completed painting through the doorway leading into the sun room, she was happy with the way it was turning out. She had spent a great deal of time fleshing out details in those rocks yesterday evening and it had paid off. She took a cup of coffee and went into the living room to spend some time in the Bible before starting her day. She started to read, but then her sister Sarah texted her.

Sarah: I'm on my way to the airport. I'll be there by two. See you soon!

Cindy's pulse soared. *What? Today, she's coming?* She thought as she peered across her living room. She saw dust on the shelves, the carpet's need of a vacuum, and her blinds that needed a good soak in the bathtub with bleach. Her sister wouldn't mind some dust and a few imperfections, but Cindy wasn't about to allow her sister to visit while the house needed cleaning this badly. Cindy texted back as she stood up and headed into the kitchen for her cleaning supplies.

Cindy: Can't wait! Have a safe trip!

Tossing her cellphone on the counter, Cindy got down on her knees and opened the cupboard below the sink. She grabbed the Pine-Sol, glass cleaner, green sponge, and a roll of paper towels. Returning to the living room, she moved each frame and book from the bookcase and wiped it all down. Then, she moved to the entertainment stand and removed any free-standing objects in order for it to be wiped down. As long as she kept moving, she'd be able to clean the house before it was time to go pick up her sister from the airport.

An hour and a half into cleaning, her daughter, Melody, called.

"So, Mom. Tell me about the retreat."

Out of breath and craving to lie down on the couch and rest, Cindy shook her head. "It was good, but I'm cleaning."

"Cleaning? Who's coming to town?"

Cindy laughed. "Why does someone have to be coming?"

"Because that's how it always is when someone is coming."

"Okay. Good point. Your Aunt Sarah is coming."

"Aunt Sarah? Wow. How long will she be visiting?"

Stopping from her current wiping of the sliding glass door, Cindy realized her daughter didn't know about the history with Sarah and Levi. She was far too young to know anything before, but now, she was a grown woman. Something in her soul held her back from spilling the dark truths about Levi and instead, Cindy kept it simple. "I'm not sure how long."

"Okay."

Cindy realized something important in that moment. She realized she didn't have to say everything to say enough. After ending the call shortly after, she lifted a prayer of thankfulness to God for the revealed truth.

CHAPTER 10

STROLLING DOWN AN AISLE IN the warehouse, David prayed for himself and his wife's situation regarding Sarah's coming to town. It couldn't have come at a worse time. They were trying to repair the brokenness in their marriage. *Lord, I don't want to be selfish, but this doesn't feel right.* Turning a corner, he started back toward his office on the other end of the building. Just then, a verse from Proverbs that he had read earlier that morning floated to the top of his mind.

TRUST in the Lord with all your heart
and lean not on your own understanding
Proverbs 3:5

DAVID'S HEART ached as God's truth pressed hard against his heart. He had to fight back the desire to take control of the unfolding situation, though he didn't want to let go. It was fine for him to lead his wife, his family, and his household, but helping someone in need for a short time was far from wrong and he knew it. Hospitality was the right thing to do, especially with Levi's past physical abuse. His heart continued his prayer. *Help guide me in the way I should go. Let me do nothing aside from Your will in my life. Please teach me.*

Just as he was about to enter the door of his office, Dean, one of the managers, stepped in front of him.

"Hey, David. You have a minute?"

"Sure, come into my office." David moved past him and opened his office door, welcoming him inside. Following behind Dean into the office, David tried to gauge what the situation was with his warehouse floor manager. Was it his wife? Family? Or was it work-related? The twenty-five-year-old appeared nervous and uneasy as he took a seat.

Arriving behind his desk, David sat down across from the kid and opened his arms wide.

"What's on your mind, Dean?"

Wiping a palm onto his jeans, the kid adjusted in his seat. "I'm a little freaked out. I found out some news the other day that has me concerned."

Immediately, David was reminded of his conversation with Mark and the buy-out. Mark had asked him to 'take some time to think about it,' and he hadn't thought even a second about it all weekend. In fact, this moment was the first time it had entered his mind since the conversation with Mark the previous week.

Leaning across the desk, David folded his hands and suspected that word had gotten out. "No decisions have been made."

Dean looked perplexed and tilted his head. "What? I'm talking about finding out my wife is pregnant with twins."

David's heart tumbled to the pit of his stomach. "Oh. Well, that's great news!"

"Wait, what is going on? You said no decisions were

made. Made about what?" Dean jumped to his feet, and concern of a different kind now intensified his already anxious expression. Dean combed his hair with his fingers and started to pace.

He couldn't lie. It wasn't the type of person David was, so he stood up from his desk and went over to shut his office door. Turning around to face Dean, he shook his head and spoke softly. "I'm sorry. Mark's talking about selling *Carlton's*. I thought word got out."

His eyes widened. "What? Why would he do that?" He paused his pacing. "Oh, jeez. Of course! And I have two babies on the way! Just great."

Closing the distance between the two of them, David brought a hand up and rested it on Dean's shoulder. He looked him squarely in the eye. "I'm not selling and that means *we're* not selling. Your job is safe, Dean. I promise."

As soon as he had spoken the words, Dean threw his arms around David and hugged him tightly. "You're a good guy, David. You know that? You really are."

"Listen, don't speak a word to anyone about this. Got it?"

He nodded, a firm smile on his face. Dean shook his head as he laughed. "My nerves about the wife being pregnant with twins have suddenly vanished! Thanks, man!"

"You're welcome. You'll be all right. You will be a good dad, Dean. And you'll love being one too."

"You think?"

David smiled at Dean. "I know it."

Exiting his office, Dean shut the door behind him. David let out a sigh, shaking his head as he sat down. He had let his lips move quicker than he should've in that conversation. Picking up his desk phone, he dialed Mark's cell.

"Hey. I'm about to walk into a meeting with Sherry's Burgers. What's up?"

"I don't want to sell."

Mark was quiet for a long moment. Then he let out a sigh. "All right."

ARRIVING HOME THAT AFTERNOON, David pulled into the driveway just shy of five o'clock, in time for dinner. Upon entering the house, he immediately caught the sound of his sister-in-law's unique cackling laugh. Taking a deep breath, David lifted a prayer to Heaven and shut the door behind him. As he walked through the foyer and into the living room, Cindy stood up and walked over to him with wide eyes and a forced smile. As she hugged him, she leaned into his ear.

"I'm so sorry. I didn't know she was coming today! I meant to text you, but I forgot to hit *Send*."

"It's okay." Her kindness softened his heart in the moment, setting his nerves at ease. As they released from their embrace, he smiled at Sarah and opened his arms, drawing her from the couch.

Sarah closed the distance between the two of them and hugged him. "I know my being here puts you out and I'm sorry about it, David."

"Oh, don't worry. You're family and you're welcome here."

"I won't be here long. I plan to find work and move out as soon as I can."

"Stay as long as you need."

She laughed as they separated from their embrace. "Let's not push it."

David sat down with his sister-in-law and wife in the living room, visiting with the two of them for the next hour while dinner cooked in the oven. As he listened to Sarah detail out the painful details of her trying marriage to Levi, it broke his heart to hear the side of a hurting wife. He knew he wasn't violent with Cindy, but the emotional turmoil sounded eerily similar. Deep down, though he wouldn't vocalize it in the moment, he knew he had inflicted some of that same emotional harm to Cindy. Every once in a while, he'd look over at Cindy as he caught sound of a familiar trait in himself. It killed him to know how much pain he had put on her in recent years. Especially when Sarah talked about the loneliness she felt when he wouldn't come home for dinners at night. Cindy, in all her kindness, stopped her sister.

"Hey, let's stop talking about this. It's sad and I'm sure it's hard for you."

Sarah nodded.

"Plus, dinner is done. Let's move to the table."

Sarah excused herself to use the restroom as David and Cindy walked into the dining room together. He came close to his wife and slid his hand against the small of her back. "I'm so sorry, Cindy."

He didn't have to explain anything more. She seemed to know what he was talking about. All those painful similarities between their marriage and Sarah's marriage to Levi.

"I forgive you."

Planting a meaningful kiss on her lips, David was overwhelmed with thankfulness for God giving him such a patient wife. As they all ate dinner, a roast along with potatoes and steamed carrots, David took notice of his heart transforming. He was able to feel his trust for Cindy returning, and though it was incremental, he was relaxing more. He wasn't letting himself focus on her mistakes but instead what he loved about her.

After dinner, Cindy and Sarah went to the mall for what Sarah liked to call *retail therapy* while David took the time to relax in front of the television. Halfway through an episode of *Gunsmoke*, during a commercial break, he remembered his desire to study more of the Bible. Inside his soul, a full-out war emerged suddenly in that very moment. On one side was his desire to seek God and on the other, his desire to relax. Finally, he grabbed the remote and shut off the TV. Kicking his recliner down, he stood up and grabbed his Bible off the bookcase and went into the dining room.

Sitting down, he jerked the Bible open but then stopped himself. *I must have the right mindset here or it won't be fruitful.* Folding his hands, he bowed his head and prayed. *God, there's a war raging in my soul right now and I need You. I always need You, but especially right now. Help me to have peace and calmness. Amen.* Turning his eyes back to the Bible, he thought, *thankfulness.* He prayed again. *Thank You for the grace You have given me. I don't deserve it at all. Thank you so much for my life. Help me to be thankful in everything and for everything.* As David finished his prayer, he became relaxed in spirit.

He started to read Paul's epistle to the church in Corinth, stopping after a passage leapt off the page to him.

What we have received is not the spirit of the world, but the Spirit who is from God,

so that we may understand what God has freely given us.

1 Corinthians 2:12

David paused and thought about the Spirit of God living inside him and the fact that he was a new creation in Christ. That had happened the moment the Lord came into his life so many years ago as a child. God had given David a part of Himself and done so freely from a place of pure and true love. The Creator and God of all the universe lived inside him, a mere man, a flawed and imperfect man. *Who am I, Lord, that you would take up residence within me? I am nothing.*

David, for the first time in his life, thought seriously about the fact that a part of God was inside him. He couldn't wrap his mind fully around the reality his mind was attempting to dwell on, but the Holy Spirit dwelling inside him gave witness to that very truth. Overwhelmed with love from God, David's eyes moistened as he felt a great sense of unworthiness. He lifted praises Heavenward and thanked God for His unending goodness to him, a sinful man. *You know my heart, Lord. You know how bad I am at moments and yet You love me, and You gave Yourself for me. Thank you.*

Cindy and Sarah arrived home late that evening. It was almost ten o'clock. David's old self, the man who lacked trust and compassion with understanding, would've been upset that he had taken off work to spend time with Cindy and she was just now strolling in late into the evening. But David didn't become upset. Truly, he couldn't even bring himself to be upset with her if he wanted to. Not after spending real quality time with God. David was starting to witness God's true power that bent David's knees in submission.

"Sorry we were late getting home. We found an awesome sale at Old Navy."

David immediately recognized Cindy's attempt to appease his old selfish attitude in life and it broke his heart for her. "It's okay. Did you get some neat stuff?"

Cindy tilted her head, appearing confused for a moment, then she proceeded to show him the items in her shopping bag. As she pulled item after item out to show him, David watched her joy-filled expression with each new piece. He could care less about the clothing. What he cared about in that moment was his wife and the fact that she was smiling. *Thank You, God, for this moment. You are good. Please keep teaching me.*

CHAPTER 11

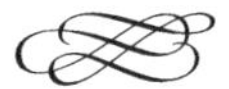

THE NEXT DAY, CINDY DROVE herself and Sarah over to Melody's house. Sarah had plans to take the car to follow up on a few applications she had submitted online the night before. Cindy wanted to take the chance to soak up as much time with her daughter before she and Tyson moved as she could. As Cindy parked in the driveway at Melody and Tyson's home, Sarah touched Cindy's arm gently.

"How much did you tell her about Levi?"

"Nothing at all. In fact, I didn't even tell her you were here to stay."

"Thank you!"

"You're welcome."

Arriving at the front door, Cindy let herself in, Sarah following behind her closely. Cindy called through the house for her daughter as she progressed further in. "Knock, knock, daughter of mine."

"Mom?" Melody's voice was distant and strained, coming from down the hallway. A moment later, she could hear Alice let out a cry. Cindy's pulse soared with worry as she hurried down the hall.

"Where are you?"

"In here, Mom." The voice sounded from the open bathroom door and Cindy rushed in.

Melody was holding Alice in her arms as she had her lowered halfway into the tub. Melody looked at Cindy with red and swollen, moist eyes. "She has a high fever and I'm trying to get it down with a lukewarm bath."

She came closer as she looked upon Alice. "How high was it?"

"103.4. I gave her Ibuprofen, but it went from 102 to 103.4 since that dose forty minutes ago."

Nodding as she knelt beside her daughter, Cindy placed a hand on Melody's back. "It's going to be okay. What about Tylenol? Did you give her any yet?"

She shook her head, tears seeping from both of her eyes. "No, the pediatrician said to wait at least forty-five minutes between the two so it's easier on the body."

"Let's get her Tylenol." Rising to her feet, Cindy hurried down the hall to the kitchen and the medicine cabinet. As she searched the cabinet, Sarah approached from her side.

"You're a good mom." Her words were genuine, filled with a sense of awe. "You always have been, Cindy. Sometimes, I wonder if I would've been a good mom too if Marla hadn't died."

Cindy stopped searching. Her heart flinched in pain upon hearing Marla's name. She hadn't heard the name in years, even decades. Her heart broke for her sister in that moment. "You would've been a *great* mom, Sarah. I know it."

Turning her head and attention back to the task at hand, Cindy finally found the Children's Tylenol and rushed back to her daughter in the bathroom. After giving a dose of medicine to Alice, they got her out of the bathtub and toweled her off. Then, they put her in a diaper and laid her down for a nap with a very thin blanket, seeing that the fever had dipped to 100 degrees. Melody made sure to turn the baby monitor on beside the crib.

Cindy walked with Melody out to the living room to where Sarah was waiting on the couch. As they entered the room, Melody opened her arms as Sarah stood up.

"I'm so sorry about that, Aunt Sarah! A sick child takes priority over *everything,* sleep and eating included!"

They hugged, and Sarah patted her back. "It is nice to see you being such a good mommy, Melody!"

All three sat down on the couch and chatted lightly about Sarah's plans to follow up on job applications and the woes of Melody's sick child over the last day.

"I know at Tyson's work, they are looking for a receptionist. If that's something you're interested in."

Sarah shook her head, frowning as she did. "I'm not really into that. I need a job where I don't see people very much. I think that's why I'd do good with something like data entry."

Cindy let out a laugh as she recalled her sister staring at the keyboard as she filled out applications last night.

Sarah pulled her head back and furrowed her eyebrows. "What's so funny?"

"Data entry?" Cindy raised an eyebrow, nodding as she tried to encourage her away from the idea. "You stared at the keyboard as you fingered each key last night filling out applications. You can't be serious."

"Of course, you don't believe in me . . ."

"Um, you need more than some people with faith in you, Sarah. You need to be realistic. Just getting a basic job, even if you have to deal with people, is a first logical step. *Anything* is better than nothing."

Sarah shrugged. "I'm really smart and I need a job that can appreciate these brains."

"True, but sometimes, you can't do exactly what you want to do. Not at first, anyway."

Sarah stood up and pushed her purse strap up onto her shoulder, then stuck out her hand. "Keys? I'm going to go now."

"Okay." Handing her the car keys, she stopped Sarah by touching her hand. "Hey. Don't be upset with me, please?"

"Be supportive and I won't be upset."

"I am supportive. Listen, all I'm trying to say is be open to other jobs. Don't neglect the future by only focusing on the present."

"What?"

"If you only think about what you want right here and now, you'll never be happy. You have to tend to the future by doing what you *need* to do today."

"Hmm. All right. I'll keep that in mind. Be back by noon."

As she walked out the door, the front door shutting behind her, Melody scooted across the couch and right close to her mom. "You should be a little nicer to her. She's trying."

"I'm trying too."

Appearing to take her mother's hint that she didn't want to talk about it, she turned toward her mother and changed the subject promptly. "Tell me about the inn. How'd it go?"

Cindy's entire being lit up as her mind shifted to the wonderful weekend with David. "It was truly a magical weekend. Your father is really different."

"From two days at a lake?"

"That's exactly what I thought too! It has to be a God thing, Daughter. Things are way too different from before the trip, and in a good way." Stopping as she realized she was speaking with her daughter, not a friend, Cindy regretted the words she had spoken. Melody didn't know about the issues in their marriage. She didn't know about the inner struggle that Cindy had faced for years. Judging by the look on her daughter's face now, Cindy quickly realized she had said too much.

"Wow, Mom. I had no idea things were that bad."

Touching her arm, Cindy attempted to reassure her. "That's all in the past and not something you need to worry about. Listen, things are looking really good for your father and me right now. Plus, you should know, Melody, that marriage goes through seasons. It's a cycle. Sometimes you aren't fighting, sometimes you are. Sometimes you're feeling like you just got married, sometimes you feel like you've been married longer than you've been alive. The reality is that marriage is hard. Paul even tells us that in the Bible. The key factor is that we love each other. You're an adult now and you have your own marriage and family. You, too, will go through difficulties."

Smiling as she tilted her head, Melody shook her head. "Tyson and I rarely ever disagree."

"You'll get there. Give it a year or a decade!"

Melody laughed. "We'll see."

THAT EVENING, as dinner was winding down back at David and Cindy's house, Sarah's cellphone rang in her purse. Thinking it might be a job, it wasn't surprising when she took the call in the other room. With her sister away from the table and it being just Cindy and David, Cindy smiled as she caught David's gaze.

"I'm sorry she's always around." She shrugged as she glanced at her plate and forked a few green beans. "It kind of takes away from our newfound time and dinners together."

"It's okay, dear." David took a bite of his mashed potatoes. When he finished chewing his bite, he wiped his mouth with his napkin and set it down beside his plate. "I have men's Bible study in an hour."

"You have to go pretty soon then if you want to make it in time."

He nodded. "Yes. I feel so exhausted from being at work all day. The Spirit is willing, but the flesh is weak. But I am excited to see what's in store for tonight's study."

"I'm sure it'll be a blessing."

Sarah walked back into the room, tears rolling down her cheeks as she did. Cindy was moved with compassion and worry for her sister.

"Didn't get the job?" Cindy asked, watching her take her seat at the table.

Sniffling, she shook her head. Sarah placed her phone on the table and her gaze was fixed on it. "That wasn't a call about a job. It was Levi."

Cindy's heart broke apart. Seeing the tears and knowing it was Levi on the phone most likely meant one thing, and one thing only—she was going back to California.

"*Sarah.*" Cindy stood up from her chair at the table and came over to her. Getting down on her knees beside Sarah, she grabbed her hands. "The paint in your room hasn't even dried and you're already leaving?"

"How can I not? He told me he loves me! He told me he *needs* me! Do you know how good that felt to hear? He hasn't said it in so long. I know it's stupid, but I am stupid."

David turned to Sarah. "You're not stupid. You only care about that loser saying it because you've been chasing love all your life. You seek love from men because your father growing up didn't show love the way God intended it."

Sarah was silent, sitting quietly.

He continued. "I've watched your father treat the two of you girls like you were worthless and had no value for decades! Not by his speech alone, but by his actions time and time again. It was wrong when you were growing up and it's wrong now. He won't even talk to you, Cindy! And it's all because of what? You decided to marry me, the guy he didn't like?" He turned his eyes back to Sarah. "Your father is a jerk, and Levi is too. It's time you heard the truth. Sarah, you need to discover real love from a real man. But first, you have to learn truth and discover the true and perfect love of God."

David stopped and stood up from his chair. "Listen to me. God loves you, God loves you, God loves you. You need to not only hear that from a father's voice but accept it and receive it. In all your flaws, imperfections, and shortcomings, and mine too, He loves us. He died for us. Sarah . . . you are *loved*."

Tears streamed down her cheeks more and she shook her head as she wiped the streams away. "I know God loves me, but right now, I need my husband! That can't be wrong in God's eyes, David!"

David was quiet for a long moment, then he sat down. "I'll say one last thing. God hates more than just divorce. He hates lying. He hates abuse. He hates injustice. He hates wrong. He hates evil. He hates evildoers. The list goes on. Now . . . I have said my peace."

Picking up his fork, he worked on finishing his plate of food. Cindy was overwhelmed by David's words. He hadn't said anything like that before to Sarah or herself, and to see him doing so now made her feel a measure uneasy, but at the same time, good. Nothing he said was wrong, yet at the same time, it invoked a flare of fear within Cindy's heart. She didn't want her sister to be mad at David or at her. But judging by Sarah's demeanor, she wasn't mad at all. She was simply shocked.

AFTER DAVID LEFT for his Bible study out at Diamond Lake, Cindy went into the guest bedroom to find her sister. As she entered, she saw a picture frame on the night stand. It was of

Sarah and Levi. They both were smiling, and it appeared the picture had been taken on a boat out in the ocean. Lifting the frame, Cindy looked at Sarah's smile in the photograph. She seemed happy, genuinely happy. But Cindy knew pictures could only hold a singular moment. Regardless of however many *good* moments they had together, Cindy feared the worst in Sarah returning to Levi.

Just then, the en-suite bathroom door opened in the room and Sarah walked out, toweling her hair dry.

"Hey." Cindy set the frame down on the night stand and turned to her. "I want to talk about your going back."

Sarah shrugged, then tilted her head as she finished drying her hair. "There's nothing to talk about, Sis. I'm going back to him. He loves me and he's going to treat me right this time. I can feel it."

Cindy pursed her lips and formed a thin line as she sat on the edge of the bed. Peering into her sister's eyes, she shook her head and spoke gently. "How do you know it's going to be okay?"

"I have hope."

It killed Cindy to know her sister was stocking all this hope into a man who had failed her time and time again. He had not only been emotionally abusive, but physically too. Looking at Sarah and seeing the determination in her eyes, the closed-off body language, Cindy knew there wasn't a word she could say in order to stop her. "When are you flying out?"

"Tomorrow at one in the afternoon."

"I'll drive you to the airport."

Sarah's phone rang atop the dresser, and she grabbed it and went back into the bathroom and partially shut the door.

As Cindy walked out of the room and shut the door behind her, she could overhear Sarah talking to Levi. "It was nobody, just my sister. I promise, Levi! There are no men here."

Her heart broke for Sarah. *How can she not see the truth of the situation?* On her way to the sun room, she unloaded her heavy heart in a prayer to Heaven. *God, break into my sister's world and help her to see reality before it's too late.*

CHAPTER 12

CHARLIE WAS ABOUT TO LEAD the group of men in a small prayer before everyone opened their Bibles to John chapter eleven where the evening's reading was located. The group was waiting on Jonathan to arrive. He had a small emergency on the home front he needed to tend to and was running a few minutes late. Besides Jonathan, the other men there that night were Tyler, Charlie, and David. Charlie had explained that his heart's mission for the group was to keep it somewhat small and intimate in order to help cultivate accountability with one another, but anyone is welcome.

Jonathan showed twenty minutes past the hour.

"Sorry about that, guys." Jonathan entered the living room slightly out of breath.

"What, did you run up the driveway?" Tyler asked jokingly.

"Actually, I did."

Everyone laughed, then proceeded to take their seats in the chairs set up in the living room.

Charlie said, "Let's pray." Every man bowed their heads,

and Charlie prayed aloud. "Lord, tonight, we will read about Lazarus. Not just a man in the Bible, but a man whom Scriptures reveal to us Jesus *loved.* My prayer for this group of men, and for this evening, is that we get out of the way and You speak directly into our lives through Your Word. Help us not merely be men in this fallen world but men of God who seek You always. We ask You to bless this time together and the reading of Your Word. Amen."

David opened his eyes as Charlie told the men to turn to John eleven. He could hear the Bible pages turning among everyone and the sound recalled to his memory the men's group he had attended years ago in his twenties. He was on fire for the Lord then, and he recalled being dependent not only on God in his life but daily readings of the Bible. A measure of guilt for losing that Godly habit invaded him. *Let go of the past,* he told himself as he picked up his Bible from beneath his chair and thumbed to John chapter eleven.

Charlie read aloud.

Now a man named Lazarus was sick. He was from Bethany, the village of Mary and her sister Martha.

(This Mary, whose brother Lazarus now lay sick, was the same one who poured perfume on the Lord and wiped his feet with her hair.)

So the sisters sent word to Jesus, "Lord, the one you love is sick." John 11:1-3

Stopping, Charlie opened it up for discussion among the men. "What jumps out at you here, men?"

Jonathan raised an eyebrow, his eyes still fixed on the Scriptures. Lifting his gaze, he surveyed the group. "Mary's experience with Jesus. This was someone who knew Jesus and had previous experience with Him."

"I agree." Tyler nodded as he continued. "She had spent time with Jesus and sent word to Him about Lazarus."

"What else?" Charlie inquired, his eyes coming to David.

David looked at the passage again, searching for something within him to add. "Um . . . they called Lazarus the one Jesus loves. So, in my mind, he was His friend, a really good friend."

"That's right." Charlie looked at his Bible, then pressed a finger against the page as his gaze returned around the circle. "These ladies sent only seven words to Jesus. The message was brief. You know, when I call upon Jesus in my own life in prayer, I can be a little long-winded. I have to give details as if He doesn't know them and then I even suggest what He could do about it."

Everyone laughed and nodded in agreement as Charlie continued.

"And you're right, Jonathan, about these ladies having experienced fellowship with Jesus. They had spent time with our Savior. And now when it's time to send a message about Lazarus, they were brief. To me, that shows *a lot* of trust in Jesus which came after spending time with Him."

David's heart opened like a rose blossoming for the first time and he felt his heart warming at the truth being revealed in God's Word. He had read this passage a multitude of times and hadn't once thought of it the way Charlie was explaining it.

Charlie paused for a moment, staring at the ceiling. Then he finally spoke. "Seven words are all that was sent by them. Here's an example of what that looks like. *'God, here's the situation in my life.'* It's an incredibly short message for something huge going on. I'm guilty of talking a whole lot more than I am trusting. If we could use these two ladies' story for a template of how to approach God with our big problems, it could alleviate a lot of heartache. Don't you think?"

Jonathan shrugged, then adjusted in his seat.

"What's on your heart, Jonathan?" Charlie asked, obviously seeing an uneasiness rise in his disposition.

"I think you're reading a bit much into this passage. Maybe they had to pay per word or something? I don't know."

"2 Timothy 3:16 tells us that all Scripture is God-breathed and good for teaching. I see these ladies purely for what they are doing in this moment. They spent time with Jesus, fact. Then they sent a short message during a time of crisis, fact. You see, when we slow down and really look at the Bible and what is really going on, we can glean a lot. I don't believe we are reading too much into this passage but instead seeing what it really says. The simple fact of this passage is that these women had a huge problem going on. Lazarus was dying, and they reached out to Jesus for help. They were brief in their communication."

"That is true, but how does that apply to us? How would we ever shorten what we are telling God?" Jonathan's face reddened a second later, obviously embarrassed by his confession in the moment. He shook his head and looked down. "Sorry."

"No, Brother. Don't be sorry. That's what this group is for. Discussion. These gals were brief, but something was in place *before* they reached out to Jesus for help. They had a relationship, a closeness with Jesus, with God."

"Yeah, I agree." David raised his eyebrows. "A lot of times, we use prayer as a last resort, and for the Biblical Christian, it should be the first thing we do."

"You're correct." Charlie glanced over at David, then continued speaking. "God has to be a priority in our life, and our relationship with God has to be a priority too. *Then* when the bad news comes, that communication doesn't have to be long because we're already in relationship and fellowship with Him."

"Wow." Tyler combed a hand through his hair. "Three verses in and I'm already blown away in awe."

Charlie smiled. "God is good."

The group continued reading the rest of the story of Lazarus, discussing and sharing their hearts and struggles along the way. After the Bible study ended in prayer, Jonathan stood in the kitchen with Charlie and chatted lightly while Tyler and David were in the living room.

"Did you have a good time tonight?" Tyler asked, glancing over at David as he put his coat on.

"I did. It seemed to tie heavily into our talk over the weekend. How we need to keep our eyes on Jesus to live good and Godly lives."

Tyler smiled. "It's all connected, Brother. How are things with the lady at home?"

David thought of his wife, Cindy, and then of his sister-in-law, Sarah, and all the drama she had brought to his doorstep. Things were going fine with Cindy, but it felt stalled since Sarah showed up. "Well, my sister-in-law moved in."

"Oh, boy."

David laughed and smiled. "It's okay now. She's leaving again. Having her around the house kind of made me uneasy and on-guard. You know what I mean?"

"Yeah, yeah. For sure. Like you can't be yourself fully."

"Exactly." David thought about Cindy. "Things are good with Cindy. Going in the right direction, at least. I hope it lasts."

"Just keep your eyes on Jesus and in fellowship with God."

"Yep." Thinking about Sarah and the fact that she was going back to California made David's stomach twist. "The sister-in-law is going back to a bad situation. You know, it's painfully sad to watch some people make the wrong choices. But I guess God did that with me for a long time."

He patted David's shoulder. "God's patience and grace are truly beautiful things to witness."

Charlie walked into the room from the kitchen, Jonathan by his side. "Listen, guys. We won't be meeting next week. I have to be out of town, but we will get together the following Thursday."

"Okay, sounds good." David shook Charlie's hand along with the others' and everyone proceeded outside to leave.

ARRIVING HOME, the house was oddly quiet. No television on in the living room, and no cackles from Sarah could be heard either. David set his keys on the kitchen counter and proceeded down the hallway to his bedroom. It was after nine thirty by the time he got home so he suspected that maybe Cindy had already climbed into bed and drifted off to sleep. Upon opening the bedroom door, he found the bed still made and no Cindy anywhere in sight. *That's odd.* He returned to the hallway and proceeded back to the kitchen, then into the sun room to see if he had missed her. She wasn't anywhere.

"Cindy?" he called out, coming back into the kitchen.

"I'm in here." His wife's quiet wounded voice sounded from the dimly lit living room. His heart ached at the sound of her distressed voice. He went into the room. Turning on the lamp beside the couch, he saw his wife's cheeks moist with tears and her eyes swollen and colored red. Moved in his heart for her, he sat down beside her on the couch and wrapped an arm around her.

"What's wrong, honey?"

Sniffling, she shook her head. "You already know."

Sarah. He couldn't do anything to help Cindy in this moment of pain. There was no way he could fix it. Pulling his wife closer to him, she lay her head on his chest and he kissed the side of her head. He searched for something to say, something that could possibly bring a measure of encouragement to his heartbroken wife. "She'll figure it out eventually, Cindy. She's a grownup and can make her own decisions."

"Why can't you ever just not speak, David?" His wife's icy words cut him deeply. Suddenly, holding her felt awkward and uncomfortable. He adjusted away from her as he let her go, his inner walls rising around his heart. He stood.

"What? Why? I'm trying to help ease the hurt you're feeling. I'm trying to help you!"

She shook her head, looking away from David. "Sure, you're trying to *fix* it. You can't fix it! I'm just sad! I just want to be held, and I want you to understand that you can't fix everything. Don't you understand that?"

David's anger warmed, and his prideful ego became offended. "Sure, I get it. You're sad, and now that I'm right and she is a screw-up, she gets to leave, and I'm stuck here to pick up the broken pieces of your heart. My goodness, Cindy! I warned you, didn't I? I warned you!"

Cindy stood up and glared at David with a pair of hurt eyes, crushing his soul to powder. "You're so unkind to me."

Walking away from him, she left down the hallway.

David combed a hand through his hair as he felt his wife slipping away from him. *If she would've just listened to me, she could've avoided all of this heartache!* He began to pace, then he heard the bedroom door slam shut. He flinched as a growing uneasiness rose up within him.

CHAPTER 13

BLINKING HER EYES OPEN THE following morning, Cindy peered next to her on the bed to see that David had never come to bed last night. Her heart ached thinking about the painful conversation they had last night. Pushing the comforter off her, she sat up and draped her legs over the bed. *I need to apologize to him,* she thought as she slipped her feet into her slippers and went for the door.

As she came out of the bedroom and into the living room, she saw a blanket and couch pillow at one end of the couch but no sign of David. Glancing out the living room window, she didn't see his car in the driveway either. He had left this morning without a word, like he used to, and dread filled her immediately.

Going into the kitchen, she poured a cup of coffee. As she grabbed the mug from the counter, she could feel her hands and insides trembling with worry. *What if I lost him because of last night?* With her coffee in hand, she headed to the sun room to paint. *If a little disagreement could launch him back into not caring, it was never real to begin with,* she thought with absolution in her mind. Setting the coffee down beside her pallet, she sat on her stool and took a deep breath and then exhaled. *Lord, help me focus and be calm.* She prayed a while longer until she was calm enough to paint. As she began to paint, her thoughts and worries melted away.

A knock on the door frame sounded a few minutes later, startling her.

She jerked around in her seat on the stool. It was Sarah.

Sarah smiled warmly and leaned against the doorway in an oversized red sweater and a pair of pajama shorts. "Don't you worry about your sister. I'll be okay."

Cindy set her paintbrush down and stood up. "But I am worried about you."

"You don't have to be though!" Sarah came closer and grabbed hold of both of Cindy's hands as she beamed. "Everything is going to work out, I know it."

"He's hurt you before."

Her smile fell away, and she let loose of Cindy's hands. "You never liked him, Cindy."

She shrugged. "He was fine in the beginning, then he hit you and did all that other junk and I can't let it go."

"Oh, *Sis*. He hasn't hit me in so long or done anything like what he did back in those days. If I, *his wife,* can get over it, can't you?"

Cindy feared saying another word, for if she said too much, she could lose her sister. Tucking how she really felt down deep, Cindy forced a smile out. "I can get over it when you put it that way. I'm here for you. Do you need help packing?"

Her sister laughed and shook her head. "I barely even unpacked! It didn't take more than a minute last night to fill my suitcase with the few pieces of laundry you had already cleaned. Hey, I heard you and David arguing last night from my room. Everything okay?"

No, things weren't okay between them, at least not right now, but she wasn't about to share that part of her life with Sarah. She had enough to worry about with Levi.

"We're fine. Hey, did you still want to see Riverfront Park before you leave? If we go soon, we can check it out."

"I'd like that."

WALKING along the bridge in Riverfront park, they stopped and looked over at the roaring falls below. Cindy couldn't stop thinking and worrying about her sister. Unable to control herself any longer, she turned to Sarah. "You'll call me if things get . . . uneasy. Right?"

Sarah came closer to Cindy and rested her hands on both her shoulders. She raised her voice over the sound of the falls as she spoke. "You and I both know that God will protect me. I am a child of God. *Plus,* I know Levi differently than you do. I know Levi is a good man. He wouldn't ever do anything to hurt me again. Those drugs made him crazy back then. He's really mellowed out, Cindy. You and David have to come visit sometime."

"We'll see."

As Cindy and Sarah continued their walk over the bridge, the sounds of the falls faded and a Bible verse pressed against Cindy's mind. *There is no fear in love.* Waiting for the courage to tell her sister the verse, they continued walking the paths in the park and then came down and around a path leading under a bridge. Cindy stopped Sarah with a touch of her hand.

"John 4:18 says, *'There is no fear in love.'* Remember that, Sarah."

"Is that what you told yourself on the nights you cried yourself to sleep about David not loving you anymore?"

A blush crawled up Cindy's neck and caused her mouth

to clamp shut. She had forgotten about the confession she had let slip over a year ago on the phone to Sarah. Immediately, Cindy felt uneasy.

"You forgot you told me about all that. Didn't you?" Sarah came closer and tilted her head. "You and I aren't that different, Sis. Sure, Levi might have smacked me around a few times years ago, but your husband has been emotionally abusing you for a *long* time. Don't be so quick to judge me when you haven't even taken a moment to look at yourself. That beam is looking mighty large."

Cindy kept quiet about God, the Bible, and her feelings about Sarah for the remainder of their time together that morning in the park. She also kept a tight lip on their way to the airport. She had no right to weigh in on Sarah and her choices with Levi. Cindy's sister might've been beaten with the fist of her husband, but Cindy had been beaten by the silence of her husband's mouth and heart for far longer.

Once in the airport and after Sarah checked her bags and got her ticket, they stopped just short of the security checkpoint line.

With tears streaming down her cheeks, Cindy looked into her baby sister's eyes. "I love you, Sarah Bear."

"I love you too, Sour Patch."

They both laughed and smiled, then hugged once more with teary eyes. As Cindy watched her sister fall into the security checkpoint line, her stomach somersaulted. It didn't feel right. Her sister returning to California, Levi suddenly giving her a call shortly after she arrived to Spokane. Something was off. Cindy resolved that she had to put her trust in God. *Help me to trust You, Lord.*

Leaving the airport, Cindy returned to her car in the parking garage alone. As she got in and started the car, she called her husband's cellphone for the first time that day. The call went to voicemail. Frustrated, she called his work and was patched through to his desk phone.

"Hello."

"Hey." Cindy's words were hesitant beyond the greeting, hoping in some part of herself that he'd apologize first. When a few moments passed without a word, she felt a deep ache in her soul. The same ache she felt for years was returning, and it fueled her anger. "What happened this morning? You left without a goodbye. We back to that, David?"

He let out an annoyed sigh. "You didn't seem like you wanted a goodbye after the way you treated me last night!"

"The way *I* treated you? You were insensitive and a complete jerk to me!" The ache inside her grew with each passing moment in the conversation. This ache was more painful than the one she had been accustomed to, and she contributed it to the fact that things had been going so well up until now. Cindy wished it never would've started to get better between her and David. At least then, she wouldn't feel like she was on a roller coaster.

"Listen, I am swamped with work. I can't sit on the phone and argue."

Her heart felt severed in half at his final words. He was blowing her off the phone and pushing her away. Typical David, but she had to try to grab hold of the situation.

"Don't push me away again, David. Please?"

There were a long few moments of silence followed by another heavy sigh from his end of the phone. "Meet me at *The Onion* in an hour and we'll have lunch and we can talk."

"Okay."

Hanging up the call, Cindy sat in the parking garage a little while longer and cried. Could her marriage ever get better? She felt too old to be dealing with drama like this. She wanted out of the drama, out of the pain, and off the roller coaster ride.

Cindy started to think about California, more specifically, Los Angeles. She had been there years ago to visit her sister for a few days. After twenty minutes more in the car, she decided a trip away would not only be a great way to get out of current situation with David for a while, but also a way to keep an eye on her sister. All that was left for her was to convince David.

TAKING their seats at the restaurant, David thanked the hostess and then turned his gaze across the table at Cindy.

"I'm sorry about last night. I know I need to be more real about how I feel, and I failed in that way, I guess. Listen, Cindy, it pains me deeply to see you upset and teary-eyed so when I found you sitting in the living room crying, I went into fixing mode. I just want to make your life as good as I can. It's the way God made me. There's a lot of stuff I have to work out within myself and in my head, and it's going to take time before it's good the way it used to be between us."

While Cindy did hear what he had to say, she was more anxious and focused on her newfound plan of visiting California. "I appreciate that, but I want to talk to you about something."

He opened his arms and raised his eyebrows. "Sure, what?"

"I want to visit my sister."

David's face grimaced. "I don't know if right now is a good time for that. We're trying to fix things in our marriage, and now you want to leave?"

"I hear that, *but* my sister is going through a difficult time."

"We're going through a difficult one too!"

Tilting her head, Cindy laughed lightly. "Come on. You know as much as I do that my sister could be in physical danger being with Levi."

"But she made the choice to go. You're not your sister's keeper."

"I know I don't have to do this, but I *want* to, David. She means a lot to me and . . ." Cindy's eyes welled with tears, memories flooding back into her mind of the pictures of her little sister with wounds all over her face and body. Her heart flinched with pain. "I feel like I need to protect her."

The waitress arrived at the table and took their orders. As she walked away, the conversation about California was forgotten by David and he changed the subject away from California.

"Mark's wanting to set up this new point of sale system that's going to eat into fourth-quarter profits. He's been acting strange for the last week or so and I think it has to do with our conversation before the inn trip."

Cindy kept thinking about Sarah in the security checkpoint line and that feeling in the pit of her stomach telling Cindy that things weren't right with the situation. She leaned on the table, her eyes wide and fixed on David. "So, would you be okay with my going to California?"

David shook his head. "You're not listening to me at all, Cindy. I'm trying to talk to you and all you're thinking about is Cali and Sarah."

A blush crawled into her cheeks as the food arrived at the table. "I'm sorry. Go on. You were saying about a conversation with Mark?"

He waited for the waitress to set their plates down before he replied. Opening his napkin, he set it on his lap. "Mark wants to sell."

"Sell the company? Absolutely not!"

David smiled at Cindy, a genuine smile that touched her heart. "You get me better than anyone else on this planet, Cindy. You know that?"

Warmth radiated from the center of her chest outward.

She loved her husband and felt loved by him once again. As they continued to eat their lunches, Cindy let go of her desire to go on to California. She resolved in her heart that her husband was right about not being her sister's keeper and that she had more pressing matters to deal with in regard to their marriage.

CHAPTER 14

A COUPLE OF WEEKS LATER, David took the day off to fix a dryer that was having issues over at Melody and Tyson's home. David had volunteered the night before when he and Cindy were over visiting. They had been visiting more often with the impending move coming soon. It didn't take more than a few minutes into David's visit that day to confirm the issue with the dryer. David had assumed correctly when he thought the heating element was out. Standing up from the back of the dryer in the laundry room, he took the heating element out into the living room where Melody was sitting on the floor with Alice.

"I was right. It was the heating element." Setting the heating element down onto the coffee table, David bent a knee beside his daughter as she peered over at him.

"I knew you'd figure it out. Tyson hasn't ever been very handy with those kinds of things."

"Some guys just aren't. It's no big deal."

She smiled, glancing over at Alice as she grabbed hold of a princess doll and moved it over to the play house. Resting a hand on her pregnant belly, she looked back at her father. "I'm going to miss having you around after we move."

"I'll miss you also." His mind shifted away from the sad topic. "Did you two make it to church this week?"

"No, Dad. I was tired, and Tyson was too. He works hard all week long and, sometimes, Sunday morning is just hard to get up."

"Sure. The Lord commands us to not forsake the assembly though, dear."

She looked away. "I don't need a preacher right now. I need my dad."

"Sorry." David halted his words toward his daughter. He didn't want to push her away, not now. "Hey, do you want me to check out the garbage disposal? It seemed wonky the other day."

"Yeah, that's fine."

David smiled and went into the kitchen. He liked to feel needed, and soon, she would be gone. Getting to the disposal, he discovered quickly that it was merely a loose nut inside. David went to the dryer and grabbed his tool box then tightened the nut in the disposal.

"Thanks, Dad."

"You're welcome. I'll head over to the appliance shop and grab a new element and get it in your dryer next. Should work like new after I install it."

Melody's eyes began to water, moving David's heart with compassion, and he moved closer to her. "What's wrong?"

"I don't know what I'll do without you, Dad."

He frowned, and a mixture of joy and sadness mingled within him. Though her words were about his handy-man abilities, he could sense the words carried deeper than just that. Setting the element down on the couch, he wrapped his arms around his daughter and held her close to him. "It's going to be okay, Mel. You'll get by without me, and if you don't, well, I'll fly out and fix whatever is wrong at your house. It would be a great excuse to see you!"

She laughed lightly as they loosened from their embrace. Smiling at her father, she tilted her head.

"You promise you'll come out?"

"Absolutely."

"Will you even come for the baby's birth in January?"

"You mean for your *son's* birth?" Melody and Tyson were not finding out the sex of the baby. It was to be a surprise, but David's heart hoped for a grandson.

Shaking her head, she continued smiling. "*The baby.*"

"Yes."

"You promise?"

It pained David to see the distrust in his daughter's eyes. He had missed Alice's birth because of work and he knew Melody was doubting his ability to leave work for not only a birth but a flight across the United States.

"I *promise* I will do everything I can to be there."

"Okay."

DAVID LEFT to the appliance store and returned a short while later with the heating element. After installing the element and testing the dryer, David reassembled the dryer and put his tools away. On his way out the door, Melody stopped him at the front door.

"Hey, Dad?"

"Yeah?"

"I love you." Melody and her father exchanged these three words often to one another, but when his daughter said it this time, he could feel it touch his very soul. He could sense a disturbance within her over the move and the parting that would be unfolding in a short time. He set his tool box down on the porch and came closer to her. Grabbing her arms gently, David peered into Melody's eyes.

"I love you, Melody. I know you're nervous about the upcoming move. It's a new city with a whole lot of new people you don't know."

She nodded, her countenance falling.

"But listen, it's going to be an adventure. I won't sit here and lie and tell you everything will be perfect, but I will tell you that God has a plan for you. He has a plan that you cannot even fathom. Mel, you are stronger than you think, and you will come out of this transition in life stronger than ever. You have Tyson, Alice, and my grandson. That's your family unit, and you will build a life together in New Hampshire. It will be okay."

A smile broke on her face through the tears and she hugged David tightly. "Thank you, Dad."

They released from their hug.

"Thank you for being my daughter. You have been a blessing in my life and I couldn't have asked God for a better child. Though I made plenty of mistakes over the years and neglected our family a lot, you came out amazing. The only way I can say that was possible is because of God."

"It was God. He was my dad when you weren't around. Wait. Sorry. That wasn't nice."

"Don't apologize. It's okay. I know I wasn't, and I'm the one who needs to be sorry."

"You're a good man who got side-tracked along the way. I forgive you and I know God does too."

"Thanks. Hey, I'd better get going. Have a good rest of your day, Mel."

"You too, Dad."

Stepping back inside her house, she smiled as she shut the door.

. . .

David arrived home to a note on the counter from Cindy. It indicated she would be down at the art gallery for most of the afternoon and return in time to prepare dinner for the two of them. He was displeased that she was gone since he was now home. There wasn't much he could do about it, so he pitched the note in the garbage and proceeded into the living room to sit in the quiet and read his Bible.

At dinner that night, he set his fork down on his plate and looked over at Cindy. "You didn't say much about the art gallery when you got home earlier. How'd it go?"

"Good. There were a few very talented artists. I told you about Heather, right? The one who paints like Monet."

"Oh, yes. She had a lot of people come by her piece today?"

"Yep. She attracted quite the crowd." Cindy rose from her seat at the dinner table and took her plate toward the kitchen as she continued talking. "Sometimes, I wonder if I would've started earlier in life like this gal, what could I be doing with my art today?"

"You know as much as I do that going down the path of 'what ifs' is not a healthy mental exercise. Listen, I was thinking . . ." Standing up from his chair at the table, David walked into the kitchen with his plate and placed it on the counter beside the sink. He turned to Cindy. "I was thinking we could go down to the gas station and get a red box and some candy tonight. Maybe have a movie night?"

Her lips curled into a smile. "I like the sound of cuddling up with you on the couch with a movie."

"Good, let's go get the supplies."

After returning home with their favorite candies, David a *Snickers* and Cindy a package of *Skittles,* they cozied up on the couch and David hit *Play* on their movie. As he held his wife close to him on the couch, David's heart swelled with thankfulness to the Lord for the newness his and Cindy's relationship had experienced over the last two weeks.

Halfway through the movie, Cindy's phone on the coffee table sounded with a notification. She peeled away from David's embrace. He paused the movie with the remote and watched his wife's face as she checked her phone. Her eyes widened, and it caused a measure of worry to creep in.

"What's wrong?" he inquired.

Tears started down her cheeks and she stood up. Without a word, Cindy started to walk out of the living room. David became confused and immediately thought someone had passed away. Rising from the couch, he followed her down the hallway.

"Cindy, what's wrong? Talk to me."

"It was Sarah, David." Her words were laced with fear, trembling as it appeared she suspected the worst. Pausing at the doorway into their bedroom, she turned to him as she brought the phone to her ear.

"Cindy, I'm sure they just got in another fight."

His wife's eyes welled with tears as she shook her head and went into the bedroom. She shut the door to the room softly as Sarah picked up and they started in on a conversation. The shut door was an easy indicator to David that he wasn't welcomed inside the room or conversation. Leaning against the wall in the hallway, David's heart continued to worry about the situation at hand. He peered up at the ceiling. *What is it, God? What has happened now? Can't we get on with our lives without Sarah interfering?*

A few minutes later, Cindy emerged from the bedroom. Her eyes swollen, tears moist on her cheeks, she shook her head at David.

"He hit her, David."

Cindy's tone revealed more than just a hit but a beating. David's heart melted, and his eyes welled with tears.

"It was *really* bad." Turning, she went back into the bedroom. He followed her inside. She immediately pulled the suitcase out of the closet and threw it onto the bed. She began to unzip it.

David rushed over to her and grabbed her arm to stop her. "What are you doing? You can't go there!"

With tears in her eyes, she furrowed her eyebrows and shook his hold from her. Turning, she went to the closet and grabbed handfuls of hangers with clothes and returned to the suitcase, placing them inside. "You're a fool, David, if you think I'll listen to you this time."

"Are you nuts? He'll be there!"

She stopped and turned quickly to David. "He's a coward! He already took off from the house."

His worry was soaring into the clouds now. He could feel himself losing his wife through the conversation unfolding. He had to stop her, end this madness. He tried to reason with her.

"But what if he comes back, Cindy?" David took a step closer to her, but she headed for the closet again. He grabbed her wrist. "You can't go there. He could hurt you!"

Shaking her head, Cindy wept. "She is my sister!"

"It's not safe."

"You're right, it's not safe. But staying here while my sister is dying by the hand of a maniac isn't much safer for me either. I have to go."

David let go of his wife and he could feel his world spinning out of control. She continued to pile clothes into the suitcase. As he watched her continue to pack, he was drained of all his strength of spirit. Then with a soft and broken voice, he pleaded. "Cindy, please don't do this."

"It's not up to you what I do anymore. This would've never happened if I would have gone in the first place."

She zipped the suitcase closed. What he had feared the

most about getting closer to his wife again was unfolding before his very eyes. She was hurting him all over again. David left the bedroom and walked down the hallway, combing his hands through his hair as he felt everything they had worked toward the last two weeks bursting at the hinges. *Her leaving would've been easier to deal with if I had kept my distance like I had done so for so long!* He felt stupid for ever beginning to trust her again, to really love her. Sitting on the couch, he prayed to God and questioned God and demanded answers. Then he wept.

Soon, Cindy emerged from the bedroom and came down the hallway. She set her suitcase down beside the opening into the living room.

"You're crying?" She shook her head and scoffed, only driving his pain deeper. "Dude, I am going to *my sister's* house. You act like I'm leaving you!"

The dagger of hurt sank even deeper into his heart, slicing open the wounds of the past. Cindy was colder than ever.

"I'm worried about your getting hurt, Cindy."

"Yeah, I am worried too, but I'm not worried about myself. Goodbye, David."

Grabbing her suitcase, she left out the front door, slamming it shut behind her. And just like that, she was gone.

CHAPTER 15

CINDY FLUNG HER SUITCASE INTO the trunk of her car and slammed it shut. Another round of tears emerged from her already burning eyes and she collapsed her head into her arm as it lay across the trunk. Her heart hurt so badly for Sarah, and her heartless husband couldn't give even an ounce of care. Cindy needed him to be understanding, to be caring about the situation, but all he could think about was himself and how it *worried* him. Taking a deep breath, she lifted her head up from her arm and expelled the air and icky feeling inside her. *You can do this, Cindy. You can be there for your sister.* Walking around the car to the driver side, she took one more look at her and David's house and then got in and left.

She called the airport on the drive into Spokane and found out there was a red eye flight to LA that she'd be able to catch if she hurried. She didn't want to wait for tomorrow. She couldn't wait. Cindy felt an unmeasurable amount of guilt on her shoulders for not acting sooner with her sister. She hadn't forgotten about two weeks ago when she had dropped her sister off at the airport. Cindy knew then that something was off. Things weren't right in the situation with Levi and Sarah. She had even gone as far as planning to get down there, but *David* had convinced her otherwise. *David* had put the brakes on what Cindy now knew was the right thing to do at the time. It was all his fault that this had happened, and Cindy's anger toward him waxed hot. He had only thought about himself and not anyone else.

By the time the airplane touched down in LA, it was two o'clock in the morning. Cindy was tired, but her resolve to get to her sister was stronger than the feelings she held of sleep deprivation. Making her way through the airport of LAX, she picked up her suitcase from the baggage carousel and caught an Uber ride outside the airport terminal. As she sat in the back seat and stared out the window in the low light of the early morning, she faded in and out of sleep as she thought of seeing her sister soon.

Her mind drifted to David once more. She knew she was better off away from him than with him if he couldn't care about others more than himself. To her, she felt all his newfound kindness and love toward her were only self-fulfilling to get what he wanted. Sarah's phone call brought into the light the dark truths about David, that he only cared about himself and wouldn't dare let go of his own interests and comforts to put someone else above himself.

Paying the cab driver outside the gate at her sister's house, she walked away from the curb and over to the intercom system outside the gate. Pressing the button, she waited for Sarah or someone to answer.

"Hey, Sis." Sarah's voice sounded through the intercom.

Cindy pressed the button. "Hey. How did you know it was me?"

"Look to your left."

Glancing over, she saw a small camera on a pole not more

than a few feet away. She pressed the button again. "Oh, wow! Can you let me in?"

A buzz sounded, then the large metal gates unlatched and opened inward. Cindy proceeded in past the gates and up the paved driveway toward the house. As she came to the roundabout, she noticed a fountain of an old cowboy holding a hat. The water sprayed from the cowboy's mouth and into the hat. The water pooled in the hat, then poured out into the fountain's pool below. Cindy couldn't help but think of the old westerns she and Sarah would watch growing up. Proceeding closer to the house, she came to a large set of cement stairs leading up to the double doors.

Sarah opened the door as Cindy made her way up the steps. As her gaze fell upon her battered sister, Cindy's heart crumbled. Cuts and bruises covered her face.

"Oh, Sarah!" Cindy closed the distance between them and held her sister close. The two of them cried for a long moment and then turned and went inside the house. Cindy left her suitcase in the foyer and the two of them went into the sitting area near the kitchen. Tears rolled down Cindy's cheeks the next few minutes as Sarah went into detail about her and Levi's latest argument. Sarah told Cindy how she had made him a lovely meal that evening and when eight o'clock came and went and no word from Levi, she called him. He rushed home, but it wasn't because he was hungry. It was because he needed to teach her a lesson about respect. He had been at a fancy dinner in downtown LA and was grooming a client for an upcoming venue at the arena. It all didn't make sense to Cindy, but then again, nothing about Levi made sense.

"I'm so sorry, Sarah." Reaching out, she embraced Sarah in another hug. "Should we go stay in a hotel?"

Shaking her head, Sarah showed no interest. "I don't think he's coming back here. This time was different than the others. After he got done and I was covered in my own blood, he had a look in his eyes like he knew. He *really* knew." Her words got choked up at this point, and she cried more, grabbing for additional tissues nearby. Shaking her head, Sarah looked Cindy dead in the eyes a moment later.

"David was right."

Cindy didn't like hearing her husband's name and the phrase 'was right' together in the same sentence. "What?"

"At the dinner table when I was there. Remember? He said I need to understand God's love before I can find a man who loves me the way I deserve. The truth is that I believe in God, go to church on Sundays, but . . . but I don't live my life for God. He isn't consulted on things in my life daily. Instead, God's more like the thing I do on Sundays. I don't have a real relationship with Him."

Cindy's anger for her husband softened. Cindy rested a hand on Sarah's hand. "God loves you, Sarah, and He has a plan for your life."

She laughed. "Yeah, right! How could He love me when I make mistake after mistake?"

"The Bible tells us that He loved us when we were still dead in our sins. Listen, God loves you, my beautiful sister, but you have to realize something." Cindy wiped her eyes of tears, then continued. "He wants a relationship with you, Sarah Bear. Jesus dying on the cross saved your soul from Hell. It is done, it is paid for by Him. You believe that and have accepted it. But now as a new creation, it's your responsibility to live out your faith. Works don't save you, but they are the evidential fruit of the transformed life in Christ. Like I just said, He has a plan for your life, Sarah. Plans to prosper you and take care of you."

"Yeah." Sarah shook her head, a sardonic laugh escaping her lips. "Really prosperous. I couldn't find a job."

"You were only in town for two days, Sis. Plus, that

doesn't necessarily indicate financially prosperous. There is more to life than the temporal. Some of the most miserable people on earth are the wealthiest, and some of the happiest are poor. The money doesn't matter. It's the relationship a person has with their Creator. He is the one who gave you the breath in your lungs. He knitted you together in our mother's womb. You are precious, and what Levi did to you is downright wrong. You can't allow yourself to go through this ever again."

As Sarah adjusted on the couch, she grabbed her side and groaned. "It hurts so bad!"

Just then realizing Sarah hadn't gone to a hospital, Cindy gently helped her to her feet. "We need to get you to a hospital."

"I can't. He'll get in trouble."

Cindy let go of Sarah's arm and turned Sarah toward her forcefully. Looking her in the eye, she shook her head. "Your time of protecting him is over, Sarah. I just flew over a thousand miles to come be with you and help you. I'm not saying that's why you need to do it. I'm saying Levi is no longer an option in your life or I'm leaving right now. You need to do this for yourself, Sarah. God loves you and I love you too. You are done protecting that scumbag, and he will pay for this."

Sarah hesitated but then nodded. "You're right. I'm done protecting him."

After spending the next hour and a half in the waiting room, they put Sarah into a room. They were sending someone to her shortly to take her for X-rays. As the nurse left the room and the two of them alone, Cindy moved her chair closer to the bed and grabbed hold of Sarah's hand.

Brushing a strand of her hair away from her forehead, Cindy smiled.

"I'm proud of you for telling them the truth about Levi during your intake."

Sarah swallowed hard and stared at the ceiling. Tears started to trickle down the side of her face. "He's going to kill me."

"No, he won't. The cops are going to arrest him, and he'll be locked up."

She shook her head. "He has money and connections. He'll bail himself out of jail and come get me!"

"I won't let that happen. *God* won't let that happen."

Turning her head to look at Cindy, Sarah furrowed her eyebrows. "Don't get me wrong. I believe in God, but I can't hide from the questions that go on in my head. Where was God when Levi was beating me? This time, the last time, every time. Where was God?"

"I'm not going to sit here and pretend to understand how God works. God didn't stop him, I don't know why, but what I do know is God didn't let you die. You survived, sister. You still have a purpose on this earth and God is going to lead you to it if you let Him."

"God lets a lot of terrible things happen to people in this world. There is a lot of hurt all over the place."

"Yes, there is a lot of pain in this fallen world, but God doesn't cause it to happen."

Sarah became louder. "But He allows it!"

Cindy thought of David, the years of hurt he had inflicted on her. Then she thought about Sarah and Levi. "God doesn't see things like we do."

"How so?"

"Well, like today. He's present in today, but He didn't go through the day like we did as we traveled along the path of time. He's always present. In tomorrow, today, and yesterday.

He has the whole picture of time all at once." Cindy started to think about the purpose behind the pain in life. "I think the more pain we experience, the sweeter the joy of the Lord is. I know that much at least."

Confused by the comment, Sarah shook her head and glanced over at Cindy. "I'm not following you."

"When things are good in every avenue of life, we can sometimes feel like we don't need God. But when things get tough, it's easy to find a Christian on their knees and talking to God. Life's difficulties have a way of bringing people to their knees."

"Ahh, gotcha."

"Mrs. Kent?" A man's voice sounded from the doorway, catching both Cindy and Sarah's attention. They looked over to see a man in blue scrubs.

"That's me," Sarah said, raising her hand a fraction from beside her on the hospital bed.

He proceeded into the room and over to her. He unlatched something underneath the bed and then pulled up the metal railing on both sides. "Time to go get your X-ray."

CHAPTER 16

DAVID DIDN'T SLEEP MORE THAN a few winks the first night Cindy left for California. He tossed and turned beneath the comforter and sheets of their bed. Stress and worry railed against his heart and mind as he thought about her traveling, thought about her being in the house where Levi could reappear at any moment. David felt he had done everything right in regard to his wife and yet this was where he was at now, emotionally drained and physically exhausted.

Kicking the blankets off at five o'clock in the morning, only eight hours from when Cindy left the house, David sat up in bed. He hung his legs over the edge and combed a hand through his hair. Exhaustion weighed heavily over him as he drew in a deep breath and let it out. *How could she do this to me?* The painful thought radiated through his being. *How could this be a part of Your divine will, God?* Finally getting out of bed, he walked out of the room and traveled down the hallway toward the kitchen. As he entered the kitchen and flipped on the light switch, he saw his Bible sitting on the counter. He had spent time in the Word last night after

Cindy stormed out of the house with a suitcase, but it hadn't done any good. *Where are you, God?* He wondered as he stared over at the Bible. *Why couldn't You help me stop her? She's in danger now.* After questioning God in his mind momentarily, David proceeded to go over to the coffee maker on the counter and brew a pot.

As he waited for his coffee, he walked over to the Bible on the counter. He thought about Job's story in the Bible and it loosened his anger a fraction. Job had gone through far more than David. Turning away from the Bible, he leaned against the counter and bowed his head as he folded his arms. *God, I know if Cindy and I would've not been working on our marriage, I could've dealt with her going to California a lot easier. Why'd you let it happen like this? I don't understand it.*

Finishing his prayer, he turned around to the coffee pot and poured himself a cup. *I'm sorry for the questions. I'm just furious, Lord.*

David set his anger aside and grabbed his Bible and read while he drank his coffee. Afterward, he got ready for the day and headed out the door, leaving behind God's truth. It was as if he hadn't read a word.

Though David had tried to drown his exhaustion in caffeine that morning, he couldn't seem to fight off the feeling of tiredness. His tiredness combined with the fact that he hadn't absorbed a single word of the Scriptures that morning manifested at work. Everyone was asking what was wrong. Jessica, the receptionist up front, stopped him and asked how she could help. Dean, one of the warehouse managers, asked if everything was okay with him.

David became increasingly aware that his home issues were officially bleeding over into his work life. This reality wasn't only aggravating to David but embarrassing as well. By the time his lunch time rolled around and he hadn't heard from Cindy, he blamed her for it all in his heart and so he left his office and stepped outside to the parking lot to call her.

"How dare you!" He fired off as she answered the phone.

She was quiet for a long moment. Then, she finally spoke. "How dare I *what,* David?"

"Only think of yourself! I didn't sleep at all last night and now I have everyone around here grilling me about what's wrong. Everyone keeps bugging me and I just can't help but blame this all on you!"

She was quiet for another long moment before replying. Then, when she did reply, she didn't acknowledge anything he had said. "Everything is going okay here. She had an X-ray at the ER last night and it turns out she has a few cracked ribs. I was surprised by it, but she's back home now and resting. With time, she'll feel better. *Thanks for asking.*"

David's frustration only grew and his anger with it. He replied harshly to his wife and said, "Oh, that's nice. Maybe she can be fully healed and ready to go for the next beating!"

Cindy hung up. Her decision to hang up the call infuriated David further. He squeezed his phone tightly and cursed. Then, he staggered his steps forward and cocked his arm back that held his phone. He almost threw it but stopped short. Relaxing, he smoothed a hand over his face and the guilt of his words and behavior overwhelmed him. *I'm acting like an idiot.* He called her back.

"Oh, joy. You again . . ."

Her words were icy, but he knew she had every right to be angry at him in the moment. "Look, I'm sorry. I am barely hanging on by a thread today."

"And you called me because why? I'm an easy target for you to unleash on verbally? You know, David, I might be able to accept your apology if you meant it, but you don't."

He shook his head, his anger inching up inside him. "An

easy target? What are you talking about? You have no idea if I meant it or not. I'm telling you I meant it!"

"Yes, yell at me as you attempt to convince me you're sorry. That makes sense. Listen, I need to tend to my sister. I'll talk to you later."

Click.

He breathed deeply and was able to control himself this time. Sitting down with his back against the wall, David set his phone down beside him and dropped his face into his palms. He felt so alone, so isolated in his pain. Then he remembered it was Thursday. *Oh, no. It's Bible study tonight.* David didn't want to tell the guys about her being gone. He took a lot of pride in the fact that that he and Cindy were in a good place the last couple of weeks and saw it as God's blessing in his life. Now with her gone, he'd look like a fool. After all, what kind of man couldn't manage his own household? For the rest of his day at work, he contemplated not going.

SPRAWLED out on the couch that evening, David drifted in and out of sleep as he watched reruns of old football games on ESPN Classic. He hadn't gone to Bible study but elected to stay home and relax and keep his business to himself. He thought the text message to Charlie saying he couldn't make it would suffice. At just shy of eight o'clock, the doorbell rang. Furrowing his eyebrows, he wondered who that could be and got up from the couch to go answer it.

To his surprise Charlie, Tyler, and Jonathan were all standing there on the porch.

"What's up, guys?"

Charlie tilted his head. "You okay, bud? Your text was vague, and we were worried."

"I'm great." David couldn't hold up the lie for very long.

Immediately, he sighed and shook his head. "Honestly, Cindy took off to California and I'm a wreck."

Opening the screen door, David let the guys into his house. He led them into the living room to sit down and then explained the situation.

"I can't imagine what you're going through right now." Charlie frowned, nodding as he did. "I'm sure it's tough. Can we pray for you, Brother?"

"Absolutely, you can."

All of the men got up and huddled in close as they bowed their heads and put their arms around one other.

"Our brother is hurting, God." Charlie paused, letting a moment pass before he continued. "David needs Your help that only You can provide. We know the truth of Your Word and the command *not* to rely on our own understanding but to trust You, God. I pray that You equip David right now to be able to do that, to trust. Help him not to lean on his own knowledge but to lean on You alone. We pray these things in Your name. Amen."

Once the prayer was over, David inched his steps toward the door, hoping to encourage the men to leave. Tyler noticed.

"Why are you trying to rush us out the door?" He smiled and patted David's shoulder. "We want to have fellowship with you."

"I'm sure you do, but I haven't slept much and I was just about asleep."

"Okay."

Charlie and Jonathan said their goodbyes to David and headed out the front door. Tyler, however, hung back in the foyer. He looked at David. "Listen, if you ever need to chat, give me a call."

"Thanks."

Tyler headed for the door, but then he turned back to

David. "Hey, I wanted to say something about this whole situation, but I couldn't find the courage to articulate it so if it comes out wrong, I'm sorry."

David's interest was piqued. "Okay. Go ahead."

"You're not worried about her . . . you know . . . ?" He was hesitant to directly ask it.

David shook his head. "Cheat? Absolutely not. I know that much for sure."

Tyler let out a relieved sigh. "Good. Then you know Cindy is going to come back. She's only there because she loves her sister."

His defenses flared at Tyler's remark and he furrowed his eyebrows as he then crossed his arms. "Yes, I understand that, but she could get hurt by that maniac."

Tyler raised a hand. "I know she could, but just think about what I'm saying. You have to have a plan for when she comes back eventually. If you just sit here and be angry toward her, it's just going to get uglier upon her return. You must be ready for her. You get what I'm saying?"

David's face softened, and he dropped his arms. "You're right. I haven't thought much about that."

Patting David's shoulder, Tyler smiled. "Have a good night, Brother. Know that I am praying for you."

Shutting the door, David walked through the foyer and into the living room, still dwelling on the fact that Cindy would at some point return home. *Then what?* The question stung to think about it for too long. David could no longer see what the future held for him and his wife. All he saw was a blurry picture of what he had hoped their marriage could be right before she had chosen to leave for California. David had lost the sense of control over his life and his marriage.

Sitting down on the couch, he bowed his head and prayed. *God, help me.*

CHAPTER 17

A WEEK LATER, WHILE HER sister was taking a nap, Cindy ventured over to the nearby art gallery she had spotted a few days ago on their way to the beach. She'd marked its location in her mind for such a time as this when she could peel away for a couple of hours. Walking in the quiet space of the gallery, she stopped and studied each piece of artwork hanging on the walls. She took time to think about each brush stroke that the artist used. As she analyzed each piece of art, she kept thinking to herself, *I could do better than these.* Stopping at a painting that detailed waves crashing along the shoreline of an open beach, she was approached by a man.

"Those waves look like you could reach a hand out and it might just splash you. Doesn't it?"

A light laugh escaped from Cindy's lips as she nodded and turned to the man. "It does. Though it's only been a week, I miss painting."

Raising an eyebrow, he turned to her. "You paint?"

Confused by the man's question, she just then noticed a

badge with the art gallery's logo and his name on it. She leaned slightly forward toward him. "Yes . . . *Bryan*."

He laughed. "Yes, I work here. I actually run the gallery. Now, back to you. Why'd you stop painting?"

"Oh, I'm not from around here, just visiting." Cindy's eyes turned back to the painting. "I'd love to sit down in the sand and paint the waves crashing in down at Huntington Beach. That golden sunset on the canvas would be beautiful."

"How long have you been painting?"

"Years."

"Have you had any of your work shown in a gallery?"

"Yes, in fact, two galleries in Spokane. Even managed to sell one piece last month."

"Wow." The man pulled a cellphone out from his pocket, then looked at Cindy. "What's your name? I'll look you up."

"Cindy Carlton, but I don't have an online presence. I doubt you'll find anything."

The man's eyes darted away, then he shoved his phone back into his pocket. "Oh. Well, you need to fix that."

"Really? You think it'd help if I was online?"

"Oh, yes! All the successful artists I know are on Instagram at the very least. The rest of the social media platforms are good too, but Instagram is where an artist like yourself can truly shine."

Cindy didn't do much with social media. She had a Facebook account but rarely logged into it. She hadn't ever jumped into the water on the whole social media craze the rest of the world seemed to embrace. The only reason she even had a Facebook account was because of her daughter signing her up for one years ago. "How does one go about doing all that social media stuff?"

"Oh, jeez." He touched his cheek with a hand as he appeared to ponder the question. Then he said, "Wait." Reaching into his pocket, he pulled out his wallet and fetched a card from it. He handed it to her. "That's Finn Oliver. He's not only an artist, but he's really tech savvy. Before he started living off his paintings, he was in social media management. He'll help you for sure . . . well, that is, if he likes you."

Staring at Finn's name on the business card, she nodded. "How much does it cost?"

"I have no idea. You'll have to talk to him about that. If you end up painting anything while you're down in California, be sure to come see me. I'm always open to new artists."

"I will keep that in mind." Smiling, Cindy shook hands with Bryan.

AFTER TOURING around the rest of the museum, Cindy plugged into her phone's GPS nearby local artist supply shops and found one only a few blocks away. She knew her and David's bank account had the money in it but didn't want to assume all the supplies needed would be okay to buy, so she called David from the parking lot of the store.

"That's fine."

His 'that's fine' didn't sound very fine. "What's wrong now, David?"

"When are you coming home? If you're buying all these paints, it makes me a little concerned. You've already been gone for a week, and I'm not trying to fight again, but I miss you."

"That's sweet, David. I miss you too." Remembering she hadn't yet mentioned to him her plans, she decided right then was a good enough time to bring it up. "We actually do need to talk about that."

"I've been wondering when you'd bring it up. When you left, you didn't mention a timeframe."

"I've been a little nervous to bring it up to you. I don't like fighting either."

"Just get it out there. What's the plan?"

"Four or five."

"Wow, really? I guess four or five days is better than another week or two. I can do that."

"Wait. I meant four or five *weeks*."

"By golly, Cindy! What on earth for?"

"Sarah is waiting for her cracked ribs to heal up a little more and for the pending sale of the house to go through. With the money, she's going to move into a place north of LA about two hours, Simi Valley."

David was quiet on the other end of the line for a long moment. He let out a sigh, then wrapped up the call. "Okay. Well, you have a good time with your sister."

His tone was somber and made Cindy uneasy.

"You sound sad."

"I am. You're my wife. You should be here with me. Hey, I have to run. Tyson just got to the house with the U-Haul, so we have to start loading it."

Her eyes glistened with tears as her heart ached. "Okay. Tell Tyson and Melody I love them."

"Will do."

Hanging up with David, Cindy sat in the car a little while longer and cried. She missed him terribly, but she still felt the desire to be in California for her sister. Lifting her gaze out through the windshield, she saw the artist supply shop. Painting always eased the pains of her heart and she was that much more eager to start painting.

ARRIVING BACK at the house a couple of hours later, Cindy set her sacks down on the counter as she called out for her sister. "Sarah, I had such a lovely time today! Well, for the most part."

There was no response from her sister, so she walked

into the living room. She glanced around the entirety of the room. Sarah wasn't lying on the couch like where Cindy had left her earlier that day. The blanket and pillow were even absent. *Hmm, maybe she took it to her bedroom?* Cindy headed down the west wing of the house toward Sarah's bedroom.

Pushing the already partially open bedroom door all the way open, she saw her sister's bed. It was perfectly made. Yet still, no sister. Worry rose within her as she turned and headed back down the hallway quickly. She had been gone for hours. Had she run off somewhere with Levi? Her mind's imagination spun out of control as she called out for her sister. "Sarah?" She called out again, her voice fragmented. "Sarah!"

"Why do you sound so upset?" A man's voice coldly sounded from the corridor that connected the two separate wings of the house. Levi suddenly emerged from the shadows, a sinister look on his face. Cindy didn't speak a word, only looked beyond his gaze for her sister. Her pulse raced as her worry climbed within her. Only a few feet from Cindy now, Levi smiled wryly. "You enjoying my house?"

Taking a step back, Cindy demanded, "Where's Sarah?"

"She's somewhere around here. Why can't you talk to me?"

Cindy wanted to tell him a thing or two but knew it could end violently if she provoked him. "I'm just here for my sister, Levi."

He laughed. "Here for what? Your sister? You already won. We are selling the house. I don't think you have to stay any longer. Or are you still here because you think you can protect her from me?" Levi took the final few steps toward Cindy. "You're scared of me, aren't you?"

A sudden emboldened state of strength came over her. She wasn't sure how, but she knew he wouldn't lay a finger on her. Her worries melted away and she looked him squarely in the eyes. "I do not fear you."

Side-stepping Levi, she headed quickly down the other wing, calling out for her sister once again. "Sarah!"

"In here." The sound of her sister's voice was muffled, and it carried through a shut door. Glancing back as she slowed her steps at the door, Cindy saw Levi still there. He was combing a hand through his jet-black hair and mumbling something to himself. His being in the house unsettled Cindy, but there was little she could do about it, but her sister could.

Twisting the doorknob, she entered the room. Her sister sat crisscrossed over near the closet. She had a box of pictures pulled out and a pile of photographs sitting on a pile in front of her on the floor. She peered up at Cindy with tears in her eyes.

"Did you call the cops?"

"I told you I'm done with him. I'm not going to push getting him in trouble. I showed him my taser when he got here to pick up his things earlier. It's fine. Listen, do you remember this day?" Sarah held up a picture in the air for Cindy to see. It was difficult for Cindy to not press the Levi issue, but she was well aware that she couldn't force her sister into doing anything. Crossing the floor over to her sister, she bent slightly over and peered at the photograph. It was a picture of their one and only family vacation. They had gone with their mom and dad to Disneyland. It was a month after Cindy had graduated high school and Sarah was only nine years old at the time. Smiling as tears gathered in her eyes, Cindy nodded. "How could I forget? It was the last time Dad told me he loved me."

Sarah nodded, a frown on her lips. "Why didn't he tell us he loved us more?"

Cindy shrugged. The mention of her father's name stung

her heart. Her father had cut off communication twenty-six years ago after she had married David, the man who would never be worthy of Cindy, according to her dad. "You're the one who still talks to Dad. Maybe you should call and ask him?"

"What ever happened with you and him? You two were close growing up and then bam! He cut you off because of David? It's just hard to understand what kind of parent can do that."

Memories flooded in of Cindy's past. It had been over two decades since it all happened, but it was a wound still present in her heart. "It started and ended with David. I remember the Christmas I brought David home like it was yesterday."

CHAPTER 18

December 23, 1991

CINDY WAS IN LOVE AND she didn't care who knew it. Traveling up the icy steps of her childhood home in Michigan that evening, she held the very hand of the man who would father her future children. Stopping short of the front door, she rested her hand on the cold golden-colored doorknob as she turned to kiss David once more. His lips were a well of love that never ran dry. She couldn't get enough of them or him. David had been the perfect gentleman to her the last four months of their relationship since they met at the fair. She knew her daddy had to like David once he finally met him. David was polite, respectful, and loved the Lord. He was the man of Cindy's dreams and now it was time to introduce him to her parents.

As her lips parted from David's lips, she caught a flicker of fear in his eyes.

"What's wrong?"

He rubbed the back of his neck and a crooked smile curved on his lips. "I'm just worried about meeting your dad. What if he doesn't like me?"

Cindy closed the gap between them and planted another kiss upon his lips. "He'll love you. He'd be a fool not to!"

David smiled, the fear subsiding in his eyes.

She finally turned the doorknob and they proceeded into the house. As they entered the living room, Cindy could barely contain her excitement to introduce her boyfriend to her mother and father. Hank smiled politely as he shook hands with David, but Rita, Cindy's mother, came in for a full-on hug.

Rita grabbed hold of Cindy and pulled her into her and David's hug. "My girl finally found a good Christian man!"

"Nobody is good outside of Christ," Hank interjected as he took his seat back on the couch beside little Sarah. Sarah moved away from Hank and focused more on her handheld video game system.

After the hugging, Rita turned to Sarah on the couch. "Don't be rude, Sarah. Put that game down and come say hello to your sister and her boyfriend."

Sighing, Sarah set her video game system down on the couch and stood up, reluctantly shaking David's hand.

"It's nice to meet you, Sarah." David bent at his knees to meet her at eye-level. "Your sister talks about you constantly at college. She tells me you can make one mean looking snowman."

Sarah smiled and tilted her head as she peered over at Cindy. "I do make a pretty good snowman, if I do say so myself."

Motioning with a hand toward the kitchen, Rita led David and Cindy into the kitchen and dining area of the house. She maneuvered over to the stove and opened the oven. The smell of freshly baking apple pie filled the air and conjured nothing but joy in Cindy's heart.

"Wow. Is that apple pie I smell?" David rubbed his tummy.

"I haven't had a fresh piece of apple pie since I was home two summers ago!"

"Why don't you see your family?" Hank's question came as he walked into the dining area and picked up the newspaper from the table.

"Dad!" Cindy chastened him. "Leave him alone!"

David raised a hand in a stopping motion toward Cindy. "It's a good question and I don't mind sharing. My mom raised me by herself for the majority of my childhood. Well, she had help from friends at the church. Anyway, she passed away from cancer two years ago."

"*Oh*. I'm sorry to hear that." Hank took his newspaper back to the living room and Cindy's face reddened as David excused himself to use the restroom. Infuriated with her father, Cindy went right up to her mother.

"What is wrong with Dad? He's being so unkind to David. He seems colder than the ice covering the driveway outside."

Rita glanced past her a moment, then back at her. Motioning her hand downward, she shook her head. "Keep your voice down. Your dad is just your dad. He acted the same way about your aunt Beth's boyfriend when he first met him too."

Crossing her arms, Cindy furrowed her eyebrows. "Do you think he hates David?"

"Don't be so extreme. He never said that!"

David came back into the kitchen and Cindy stepped away from her mother to talk to him near the back door outside. Her voice quiet, she apologized for her father.

"It's okay."

Sarah wandered up to the two of them a moment later. "Hey, my batteries died. You want to go play outside?"

Cindy declined. She had plans to confront her father about his behavior. "No, I'm okay. But you can if you want, David."

He laughed. "Thanks for the permission. I am interested in seeing your snowman skills. Let's go."

Sarah and David exited out the back door while Cindy made her way to the living room. In her mind, Cindy hoped to convince her father how great of a guy David was and hopefully speed the warming up process between her father and boyfriend.

Standing in front of his chair and his raised-up newspaper, Cindy waited for him to lower it. When a few moments passed and he hadn't, she cleared her throat.

"Hey, Dad?" She made sure her tone didn't reflect the annoyance she felt inside. He was a man with a short fuse and he could turn rather quickly on someone if he didn't like their tone or choice of words in a conversation.

Finally lowering his newspaper, he set it on his lap. "Yes?"

"I want to talk to you about David. I get the feeling you don't care for him much—"

"Let me stop you right there. You're right. I care about my family, and that boy isn't my family. Therefore, I don't have to care about him."

"Yes, but he will be family someday."

"He has to earn the right to be called family. I'm not giving out my blessing on just any chap you bring through that door."

"But you gave it for Billy Ray."

He paused before responding. Anger flared in his eyes. "How dare you talk to me like that! I am your father. Is that college corrupting your mind already? Looks like they don't waste any time in brainwashing you."

"What are you talking about? Billy Ray is the pastor's son and you were trying to get me to go out with him my senior year! You loved that guy."

"Yeah, so what? He was a nice boy and I still talk to him

and think he's a fine fit for you. I don't know this kid, David. All I know is he has hormones."

Cindy's heart splintered. "How can you be so heartless, Dad? I love him."

"You don't know what love is. You go raise two daughters and go through twenty years of marriage, then you can talk to me about *love*."

Cindy's heart broke apart at hearing his vile reply and she shook her head as tears welled in her eyes. Turning around, she left out the back door of the kitchen. As she approached David and Sarah out in the snow, he lifted his gaze and smiled at her. When he saw her upset and crying, his smile quickly faded, and he rushed through the snow to her. He threw his arms around her and held her close, kissing her and loving her.

"What's wrong, Cindy?"

Shaking her head as tears fell onto his jacket, she felt an aching in her heart. "My *dad*."

"Whatever it is, I'm sure it's just because you're his daughter and he loves you."

Cindy didn't respond but took comfort in David's embrace, just holding onto him as the man she knew as her father shifted from a hero to a villain.

SNACKING on apple pie and vanilla ice cream that evening around the dining room table, Cindy noticed snow beginning to fall outside the dining room window. The tiny snowflakes caught the light coming from the porch. Her heart warmed. Looking over into David's eyes, she caught his gaze and a feeling of home washed over her. She knew her new home was in those eyes and she'd be there for the rest of her life. Peering over at her dad a moment later, she saw a grimace on his face as he finished his bite of ice cream and then stood up and left into the kitchen. *How can a man of God seem so miserable?* she wondered to herself.

Her mother, Rita, stole her attention. "What do you study at school, David?"

"I'm a finance major. It's all about the numbers for me."

"That's exciting. Did Cindy tell you that her father used to work in finance?"

"It was hardly finance, Rita," Hank's voice carried from the kitchen. He walked back into the dining room and sat in his chair at the table. "I worked in the finance office of a car lot."

"Don't downplay it, Hank." Rita looked again at David, then over at Cindy. "He loved that job and helped a lot of people get into cars. Isn't that right, Hank?"

"Yes, that is correct. Probably a little too much *help*." He let out a chuckle, letting his knuckles graze just beneath his chin. "That was a long time ago though. Cindy was only ten years old when I worked at the car lot. I work as an elder over at the church now. I help with the finances there some, but not a whole lot."

"That's awesome." David nodded and asked more questions about his work with the church. It warmed Cindy's heart to see the two of them finally talking, and a glimmer of hope sparked in her heart for the two of them. Maybe they could not only tolerate each other but become friends in time?

After everybody finished their dessert, it was time for bed. Rita pulled linens out from the closet in the hallway and laid them on a couch for David. David was in the bathroom showering, and both of her parents were with Cindy alone in the living room.

"You're sleeping in with your sister." Hank crossed his arms. "Your room has turned into the storage room since you left."

"I could move the boxes and clear a space for myself."

Rita smiled grimly and touched her daughter's arm. "*Cindy*. Your father and I believe it's best this way. We don't want to worry about you two."

Cindy nodded in respectful agreement even though she knew nothing would happen. David wasn't interested in anything happening between the two of them outside of marriage. It took him a month to simply kiss her on the cheek.

Hank stepped closer, glancing over his shoulder toward the hallway and bathroom where David was still showering. He lowered his voice as he spoke to Cindy. "There's something about that guy I don't like."

"Daddy. You don't even know him."

"It takes three seconds to get a good feel for a guy, and this guy . . . something isn't right there, Daughter."

Cindy's heart broke at his words. Shaking her head as her cheeks moistened with tears, she sniffled. "I love him, Dad. I'm going to marry him if he asks me."

"Not with my blessing, you aren't."

Clenching her jaw, she loathed his cold and senseless position. "You claim you love me with your mouth, but your actions speak otherwise."

Her father's face reddened and his voice grew louder. "Why don't you try having a child and raising one and then you can come tell me how it is!"

"Sure, leverage your age and experience against me again. I get it. I'll never be as old as you. So, I should just blindly trust whatever you say?"

"Absolutely. I am your father!"

Cindy shook her head slowly as Bible verses climbed to the tip of her mind. "1 Timothy 4:12, 'Don't let anyone look down on you because you are young, but set an example for the believers in speech, in conduct, in love, in faith and in purity.' Or did you only want me to memorize that Bible verse for when it suited you? Here's another verse for you, Dad. 'Knowledge puffs up, love builds up.' I love you, Dad, but your pride is clouding your judgment."

"How dare you."

Her heart was disappointed in her father's hypocritical words, and she tried to walk away, but he grabbed her arm. She glanced down at his wrapped fingers around her arm, then at him. Just then, David came into view behind Hank, catching her attention. She pulled her arm away from her father and walked past him.

"Goodnight, *Dad.*"

David turned and followed Cindy down the hall and around the corner. She stopped at her sister's bedroom door. She was in tears and sniffling.

"Talk to me. What's going on?"

Her eyes were red, her heart broken. Glancing toward the hall leading to the living room, she shook her head. "My *Dad.*"

David came closer and pulled her into his embrace. Holding her against his chest, he kissed the top of her head.

"It's going to be okay, Cindy. Everything is going to be okay."

"I know it will be, but I feel as if I just saw my father for the first time."

CHAPTER 19

ANOTHER TWO WEEKS PASSED AT home without Cindy, and the emptiness David was feeling wasn't just from an empty house. In addition to his wife still being gone, his daughter Melody and her family had left for New Hampshire. His time in prayer and Bible reading had increased ten-fold in the passing weeks, but David's soul still longed to be near his wife, to smell her scent, to feel her skin against his, and most of all, to experience her presence when she walked into a room he was in. Distance truly made David's heart grow fonder, and he was coming to the end of his ability to go on any longer.

Rubbing his forehead as he sat at the kitchen table one October morning drinking his cup of coffee, Cindy came to his mind. *Still three more weeks to go . . .* The thought ignited his anger and he closed his Bible with a snap. Standing up, he took his cup of coffee and dumped the rest out in the sink. Resting both of his hands on the counter, he lowered his head and prayed. *God, give me strength for today.*

Walking out of the kitchen, he headed down the hallway toward his bedroom to get ready for work. He had an early morning meeting with Mark at eight o'clock to go over the results of the newly implemented point of sale system they installed a week ago.

David arrived thirty minutes past eight o'clock due to a blowout on the freeway on his way into town. As he walked in, Jessica, the receptionist in front, stood up immediately.

"Is there anything I can do to help?"

He shook his head and continued toward his office. Glancing down as he walked, David saw the smeared black streaks from changing the tire down the front of his white button-up shirt. He was stopped by Dean, who asked what happened.

David flashed a polite smile. "Blowout on the freeway. Lovely start of the day."

"Whoa, man. I'm sorry!"

"It's okay." David recalled the second annoyance on the freeway. "Then there was a huge slow down on traffic as I got further up the road. Big wreck, multiple cars. It was a mess."

"*Wow*. God's got your back, man!"

David paused at Dean's words. He hadn't thought of it like that and it made him smile. "You're right. He does. I would've been in that wreck. Wow."

"By the way, I just saw Mark head into conference room. He was asking where you were."

"Okay. Thank you."

Continuing to his office, David took his blazer off and tossed it onto the chair in front of the desk. Grabbing a moist towelette from a drawer in his desk, he tried to lessen the dark smudges on his shirt. Just then, a knock came on his door and Mark entered, shutting the door as he entered.

"Sorry about the delay. I was just about to head over to the conference room. I had a blowout on the freeway."

"It's fine. Listen, I want to talk about selling again."

Stopping his swipes to clean his shirt, David crumpled up the towelette and pitched it into the garbage can beside his desk. He rested a hand on his waist as he was irritated that the topic had floated to the surface again. "I thought we already talked about it, Mark. I remember saying I'm not interested. What happened to that?"

"I know, and I remember. That's why I'm selling *my* portion of the business. I found an interested buyer."

David shook his head, a sense of betrayal filling him. He locked his eyes on Mark. "You want me to just go into business with a stranger? You think that's a good idea?"

Mark shook his head. "I've checked this guy out. He's legit. It'll be a good fit for you, I'm sure of it."

"What? You're dropping an A-bomb on me here, Mark."

"No, I'm not dropping an atomic bomb on you. He wants to buy your portion of the business also. The number he quoted me would mean a healthy retirement for both of us."

Mark pulled a pen from his pocket and a business card. He wrote down a number and handed it to David.

Raking his hair back with a hand, David sat down behind his desk. It was a substantial amount of money and would not only take care of retirement but his grandchildren's college tuitions. Shaking his head as David recalled how much he loved his work, he looked back at Mark. "I can't sell, and I can't believe you are, man."

"Well . . . get to believing it. It's happening."

A brief moment of quiet filtered through the room. With Mark still standing in the office awkwardly, David rose to his feet and went and opened the office door.

"You should try to embrace this, David. You and Cindy could travel and do whatever you want for the rest of your life. At least think about it."

David nodded slowly. "I'll think about it."

"Okay." Patting David's shoulder, Mark smiled. "Regardless of what you decide, you've been a pleasure to work with, David."

"Thanks."

Shutting his office door, David walked over to his desk and sat down. *I need to talk to Cindy about this.* He longed to share this big news with his wife and discuss the possibility of retirement but calling her didn't sit well with him. Glancing at his cell phone, he saw a missed text from Tyler. It was in regard to their plan to meet up for dinner across town later that day. Tyler had to cancel and asked if David wanted to meet for coffee instead an hour later. He hesitated and felt tempted to call the meeting off with Tyler, but he chose to keep it instead. He knew fellowship with a fellow brother in Christ was what he needed even if it felt contrary to how he was feeling.

David: Yes, coffee sounds good. I'll meet you at Milo's downtown at 7 o'clock.

His office door opened. Peering up, he saw it was Dean.

"Hey, boss. Luis went home sick and we have a *huge* shipment arriving in twenty minutes."

"I'll be down at the bay in ten."

Dean smiled and thanked him, then left his office, shutting the door as he did. As David remained sitting at the desk, he took notice of how he immediately jumped at the chance to help. Mark hadn't ever been like that. Feeling conflicted in his soul about selling along with Mark to this new guy, he decided to go to the One his life belonged to, so he bowed his head and prayed to the Lord. *What do you want me to do, Lord? What is Your will?* No clear answer rose within him, so he rose to his feet a moment later. He exited his office and went over to the break room to grab a water bottle before heading down to the bay.

. . .

The smell of slow-roasting coffee beans engulfed David's senses as he walked into Milo's that evening. He hadn't been to the little coffee shop downtown in years. Spotting Tyler over near a window, David ordered his coffee and then took it over to the table. He sat down in the metal chair with a heavy, but relieved sigh.

"Long day?" Tyler inquired.

"Amen to that, Brother." David took a sip of his coffee and set it down on the table. "Had someone call in sick so I threw freight for the first time in I don't know how long. Felt good though, you know? Oh, I also found out today my business partner is selling his portion of the business. He wants me to think about selling too."

"Wow. Are you going to?"

"I don't know yet."

"What's Cindy say about it?" Tyler raised an eyebrow as he took a drink of his coffee.

David shook his head. "We talked briefly about it weeks ago when he wanted to sell together, and she didn't want me to, but we haven't talked since he decided for sure to sell his half. It's not really the type of conversation to have over the phone."

"So, tell her in person."

"I'm not sure I can wait three weeks to tell her. These kind of business deals go quick. It's like a bandage coming off. It's better to go fast."

Tyler nodded, then set his coffee off to the side as he scooted closer to the table and leaned in. "Can I be candid for a moment?"

"Absolutely."

"I would've beat her to the airport if that was Olivia going to take a flight out of town." Tyler raised a hand. "I know I haven't been married as long as you have, but man . . . I couldn't do it. It's been two weeks and you have to wait another three weeks? This is your *wife*. I hope I'm not being offensive here with what I'm saying."

Tyler wasn't being offensive at all, in fact, he was helpful. Though it was painful to hear how he had done things incorrectly by Tyler's standards, he knew it was from a place of brotherly love. Tyler was a kind heart and truly a brother born in a time of adversity. David took a few moments to let his friend's words of wisdom trickle through his mind and drip into his heart.

"You're not being offensive at all, Tyler. You're being honest. The Scriptures say open rebuke is better than secret love, and right now, you are loving me by telling me the truth. I need to go to my wife."

"You took that better than I thought you would."

David furrowed his eyebrows as he flashed a look of confusion. "Than you thought?"

"I've been trying to figure out a good way to tell you that for a week and a half now. Finally mustered the courage." Tyler laughed and sat back in his chair as he took another drink of coffee.

"Wow." David nodded slowly as he continued. "Well, I think God had it come out right when it did for a reason. It was the perfect response to what's going on at my work."

"God is good, ain't He?"

"Amen."

Tyler glanced at a gentleman as the man walked by their table. The man appeared to be homeless judging by his ratted clothing and nappy hair. Tyler's eyes were fixed on him. "I have some news of my own. It's been laid on my heart, I feel by God, to start a home for people who need a second chance at life."

"A second chance? A home?"

"Yeah, drugs, divorce, whatever. It'll be dedicated to helping people. Assisting them in finding work, a place to live and so on. I've been praying for about six months about it and I'm just waiting for the pieces to line up now."

David nodded, imagining the place in his mind. "So, it'll be like a shelter?"

"Yes, but more Christian-based than the shelters you find around town. Church services daily, small groups, counseling. I have a few guys interested in helping get it going, and Jonathan and I are putting in most of our savings for startup costs."

"That sounds awesome, Tyler."

"I know, and I'm excited. I'm scared too. Scared to fail. I think that's how God likes it, though. That way, we rely on Him to get through it."

Nodding, David thought about going to California. It'd be a bold move on his part and scary too, but he knew seeing his wife was what he wanted. That evening, David arrived home and set forth a plan to go to California. He didn't call Cindy but instead texted her and asked for the address. He made up the excuse that he wanted to send a housewarming gift to Sarah for the new apartment she was moving into in three weeks. That evening, after he packed his suitcase, David climbed into bed and was able to sleep fully through the night for the first time since Cindy left.

CHAPTER 20

WHILE PREPARING BREAKFAST ONE morning at Sarah and Levi's house, Cindy's cellphone buzzed across the counter. Setting the spatula down beside the pan of eggs, she walked over to go answer it.

"Hello. This is Finn."

It took a moment for the name to register, but then it clicked. It was the man who could help her with her online presence as an artist. She had called him over two weeks ago and hadn't heard a word back after leaving a voicemail. She had almost completely forgotten about the man.

"Oh, yes! I remember now. I called you a couple of weeks ago."

"Yes, that's right. I'm *extremely* busy and I just now had a free moment. What can I do for you?"

"I need help setting up an online presence. I'm a painter."

"Are you serious?"

Her cheeks turned red as a cherry and her insides felt shaky. "Well, yes . . . I am serious."

"No, honey. I mean are you a serious artist? Are you in it

for the long haul? I don't work with people who don't take their work seriously, and I have little patience for amateurs."

She was confused by his words, but she dared not ask for clarification. The man already seemed annoyed and impatient and they were only a few moments into the call. *He must be good,* she thought.

"Well, I've been featured in two art galleries in Spokane and have painted for about two decades."

"Great. Can you meet me at El Carnadio's Cafe and chat about a plan at say, one o'clock?"

"Sure." She found a pen on the counter and a slip of paper. "What day?"

"Today."

Her pulse raced at the anticipation building inside her. "Yes! I'll be there."

"Fantastic."

Click.

A grin from ear to ear formed on her lips as she set her phone down on the counter. Sarah called out from the couch in the living room. "Who was that, Sis?"

Returning to the pan on the stove, she pulled the pan with the eggs from the burner and placed a lid over it. Then she went into the living room. Entering, her sister's eyes widened, and her face lit up.

"You look happy!"

"I am! That was Finn. That guy I was telling you about who I called from the business card. Remember that?"

"Wow, he finally called?"

"Yes. He requested to meet me at one. I'm not sure what we will talk about. He did mention making a plan."

"What do you have to take with you?"

Cindy shrugged. "I don't know. I'll probably bring my portfolio book."

"You didn't ask exactly what he wanted?" Sarah tilted her head, confusion littering her expression.

Cindy shook her head. "I was scared to. He sounded impatient and irritated on the phone."

"He must be good!" Sarah laughed.

"That's what I thought!" Cindy smiled warmly as she took a seat on the couch beside her sister. "I wonder if he'll like my work. I'm sure living and being in the LA art community is a far different spectrum from little ole' Spokane."

Sarah placed her arm around Cindy's shoulder and gave her a squeeze. "He's going to love your work! I just know it."

The bell on the monitor for the front gate chimed from across the living room. Sarah stood up to go see who it was. Cindy went into the kitchen to dish their breakfast onto plates. As she scooped the eggs onto each plate, she could hear Sarah walking into the kitchen behind. She turned toward her.

"Who was at the gate?" Cindy asked.

Raising her eyebrows, she smiled. "Someone for *you.*"

Confused, Cindy handed her sister her plate and headed through the house to the front doors with her own plate of eggs still in hand. Opening one of the double doors, she walked out and shielded her eyes from the California sunshine to see a man walking up the driveway. It took only a second, and then she recognized him. It was David. Her heart dipped into her stomach and fireworks exploded inside. Shuffling her feet down the steps, she sprinted with her plate of eggs past the fountain and out to meet him. Arriving to his open arms, she threw her plate into the gravel and put her arms around him.

"David! You're here!" She squeezed him tightly as she inhaled his familiar scent she had longed to smell again for weeks. She didn't know why he had come, but she didn't care. She was too happy to see him.

"Those looked like perfectly fine eggs you had in your hand." He laughed lightly and so did she, then he planted a kiss on her lips. They then walked together up the driveway toward the house.

Cindy glanced at his hands and then her gaze fell on his eyes.

"Where's your suitcase?"

"I checked into a hotel before I came over."

As her emotions settled from the excitement of David's arrival, questions began to surface in her mind. "What's going on? Why'd you fly out?"

She studied him as he searched for a response. His lips were hesitant, but then he smiled as he stopped his steps. "There are two parts to that answer. One is I've been missing you like crazy."

"And what's the other?"

He glanced away, then back at her. The anticipation sent her pulse skyrocketing. "Mark's selling."

Knowing how much the business meant to David caused her heart to break. "What? I thought you two talked about it and you told him no?"

"I did. But I can't stop him from selling his own portion of the business."

Seeing her husband's eyes glisten with the pain she knew was in his heart, Cindy reached out and touched his arm lightly. "I'm sorry, David."

David peered down at the cement beneath his feet for a moment. "He said the buyer wants to buy me out too. It'd be a lot of money. I mean, we'd retire well-off and Alice and the new baby would have their college educations paid in full. It's substantial."

Cindy took a step closer and grabbed David's hand. His gaze lifted to her. "Is selling what you want to do, David?"

He shrugged. "I wanted to talk to you about it."

"I'm okay with whatever you decide. *Carlton's* has been your passion for a long time. I'm a hundred percent behind you."

He nodded slowly, then raised his eyebrows. "So, if I stay, you're okay with it?"

"Yes, of course."

David broke into a smile.

Tilting her head back toward the house, Cindy matched his smile. "C'mon inside and I'll make us some new eggs."

At a quarter to one o'clock, Cindy dropped David off at the art gallery where Bryan had placed a few of her recent California paintings on display. He wanted to see it. On the short drive to El Carnadio's Cafe, Cindy focused her thoughts and attention on presenting herself to Finn. She had one shot to impress this guy and she hoped to gain his services to help her career as an artist take off. Parking in a stall at the café, she checked her phone. *Good, a few minutes early.* She checked the mirror to make sure she looked presentable and then bowed her head in prayer. *Lord, help me nail this meeting with Finn. I really need this chance as an artist. If it's not Your will, let it fade away and stop here.*

Cindy reached over and grabbed her iPad off the passenger seat beside her. On the iPad were not only recent works from her time in California but also images of prior work done in Spokane. That little device held her entire art portfolio.

Getting out of the car, she walked into the cafe and searched the tables for someone who could be Finn. Arriving out onto the patio area, she spotted a sharp-dressed man with a perfect jawline and haircut to match. *That must be him,* she thought and proceeded toward the table.

"Finn?"

He stood up and smiled, taking a slight bow as he did. They shook hands.

"You're ten minutes early. Good. Have a seat."

They both took their seats and then Finn browsed through her work on the iPad. He studied some of the images and quickly skipped over others. In all, it took about five minutes of browsing in silence. He handed the iPad back to her.

"We can work together. Now listen." He reached over to his left side and pulled out a laptop. He powered it on and then flipped the screen toward her to see.

"*Cindy,* let me show you what I can do for you."

For the next forty minutes, Finn went through five different client profiles on social media platforms. He talked about post engagement, Twitter followers, and Instagram stories. Cindy did her best to retain the information overload, but he assured her that he'd email her the details and teach her *everything* along the way.

"I don't do this for you forever, Cindy. I do this in the beginning and I teach you. I believe the best service people teach their clients."

"Don't you lose money if you do that?"

He shrugged. "It's about helping people more than anything else."

Closing the laptop, he returned it to his bag and then looked directly at Cindy. "You're an artist. I'm not just saying that. It's a fact. I'm not a very nice guy and I have a very critical eye for art. You have what it takes."

Cindy's heart and lips curled into a smile at his words, but he raised a hand.

"Don't let that go to your head. I have bad news for you. You're old."

A piece of her heart chipped at hearing the comment, but Finn noticed her displeased look and reached across the table and touched her hand. "It's actually not a super bad thing, it just means all the other artists who are younger have a leg up on you when it comes to technology. Being good with a paintbrush is one thing, but getting eyeballs to see your painting is another."

"I thought that's what galleries were for?"

"They are, but young people aren't in galleries. They're scrolling Instagram and checking their Snapchat. You can do this, Cindy, but it's going to take a lot of work. You will hate me for how much I make you work, and you'll probably even ask me what you're paying me for."

Payment. Cindy had forgotten about that. "Speaking of, what's the cost?"

"I don't have set prices. Each artist needs something different. Now that I've seen your work, I can start on a quote. I'll email you the details." Finn stood up, and pulling his laptop case from the floor, he swung it around his shoulder. He then asked for her email address and plugged it into his phone.

"We're not having lunch?" Cindy asked, glancing around as he returned his phone to his pocket.

"I have to go. Look for the email from me tonight. You really are talented and I'm excited to see where we can take your career as an artist."

As he left the table and the cafe, Cindy could still hear Finn still saying those four words. *Career as an artist.* She hadn't ever thought of her art as a career until now.

CHAPTER 21

As DAVID PERUSED EACH OF Cindy's paintings at the art gallery, he began to realize she was doing just fine without him in her life. This fact created within David a sense of guilt over wanting her home. Setting aside his feelings, he continued to find painting after painting of his wife's. He liked each piece of art, but one in particular caused him to pause and reflect when he came to it. It was a painting of an ocean, and there in the midst of the stormy sea was a life saver. The life saver appeared to be tossed to and fro by the waves. He couldn't take his eyes off that lone life saver. Though it was just a painting, David couldn't help but let his mind wander as he stared longer at the painting. He imagined a wreckage somewhere off in the distance. The chaos that ensued, the panic-stricken crew. There was someone on that boat who needed that life saver, and they never got it. Here it was, floating casually up and down with the waves, out of sight of the person it was intended for. It invoked a bit of fear in David.

"It's a beautiful painting. Isn't it?" A man's voice sounded softly from beside him. David hadn't known anyone was standing behind him and it jarred him out of his imagination. He turned toward the man and nodded as he smiled.

"My wife painted it."

The man's eyes widened. "Cindy is *married?*"

David's heart panged, his shoulders slumping.

"Oh, I'm so sorry! I just didn't know she was married. She didn't mention you and doesn't wear a ring. Anywho, I'm so glad to meet you! I'm Bryan."

The twenty-something-year-old struck out a quick hand to shake David's. As he shook hands with a man who knew his wife, he turned his eyes back toward the painting on the wall. The picture was beginning to become clearer, but not the painting. While he felt himself rotting away in Spokane and waiting for his wife's return, she had been in California, carrying on life on a grand scale without him. What hurt the most for David was the fact that she didn't appear to need him. She was fine without him. While he knew it was his own fault from the years of neglect of his marriage, that fact didn't make it hurt any less.

"Your wife is a very talented artist. I think she's going places in her career. People who come in here absolutely *adore* her work."

"She is good."

"Oh, she's fabulous!" As he finished his compliment, the front door of the gallery chimed as someone entered. The two men turned their gazes to see who was walking in. It was Cindy. Relieved she had returned so quickly, David walked over to meet her. Bryan followed close by.

"How'd it go with Spin?"

"Finn." She smiled and let out a relieved sigh. "It went great! He is taking me on as a client. He's working on a proposal to send over this evening."

"Girl!" Bryan smacked her shoulder. "You got Finn! Do

you know how big this is? He's going to make you a shooting star in the LA art community! I'm so happy for you!"

They hugged and danced a slight jig in the gallery. As David watched the two of them, his heart felt disjointed while he felt out of place. It didn't seem to him that he belonged in that conversation or even in the city. Walking with Cindy down the street back to the car a short while later, David glanced over at her.

"You've really embraced staying here with your sister."

Cindy nodded gently. "I just missed painting a lot and the ocean is an *ocean* of inspiration. My arthritis is better in this climate too."

"Good." David forced a smile, but he wasn't happy. He wanted her back at home with him, and flying out to California had only seemed to intensify his desire for her to be home. He didn't want to leave without her, but he also wouldn't mention it to her either. He had spent enough time in their marriage trying to tell Cindy what he wanted and being rejected each time. It was time for him to let go. After all, she was happy, and isn't that what he's always wanted for her?

THAT EVENING, they ate at a fine dining seafood restaurant that sat on the end of a pier. The atmosphere of the restaurant was warm and luxurious. A dark setting with low lighting gave the establishment both the feeling of romance and privacy. The waiter pulled out Cindy's seat for her and then went over the wine specials for the evening. Cindy and David both declined and went straight to the menus. It had taken over an hour and a half to finally get a table, so both of them were famished.

Peering over his menu, David stared over the top of it at his wife for a moment. His eyes traced her exposed neck and the top of her sun-kissed shoulder. She looked beautiful. Cindy was wearing a black and white dress, black pumps, and a white gold chain necklace that he had given to her for their tenth wedding anniversary. Overwhelmed with love for his wife, David continued just looking at her until she finally caught him.

"What?"

"You look lovely tonight, dear."

Her lips curled as she tilted her head and her eyes went back to her menu. "I love you, David."

"I love you."

The waiter arrived a moment later and set a basket of warm bread down with a plate of butter and a knife. "I'll be back shortly to take your orders."

As he walked away from the table, a violin and a Cello began to play softly from across the restaurant. The music floated gently through the air and set David's entire body at ease.

"You're loving this place, aren't you?" Cindy commented as she plucked a roll from the basket and buttered it. "Secluded in public with a violinist playing."

"You know me perfectly." Finally deciding on what to eat, David shut the menu and set it aside. "Honey. I want to talk to you."

Her gaze lifted, and she folded the menu and set it down. "Okay."

"I was a fool to ever treat you the way I did in our marriage. It's sad to say, but it's taken the last month for me to figure out just how badly I messed things up in our marriage."

Her eyes glistened and she lowered her head.

David heard the song change to a slow dancing tune and he stood up from the table. Holding out his hand to Cindy, he waited. Lifting her gaze, her eyes widened, and she placed her hand in his and he took her by the hand to the dance floor. Placing one hand on her side, he took her other hand in his and danced with her. David swayed to the music and stepped perfectly as he led his wife in a dance. Cindy eventually rested the side of her head against his chest as they slowed even further in their pace. "You remember, David, when we'd go out dancing before Melody?"

David smiled, recalling fragmented memories. Cindy was happy then, just like she was right now in California. She smiled and laughed a lot back in those days. As David continued to dance with his wife, he began to wonder if this California life was what she truly wanted. He prayed it wasn't but feared it might be.

The song ended and the two of them walked back over to the table. David sat down at the table while Cindy went to use the ladies' room.

Cindy's phone buzzed inside her purse. David heard it. He recognized the sound and knew it was her email. Remembering that Finn would be sending an email, he got up and retrieved the phone from her purse. Sure enough, it was an email from Finn. It detailed out not only the cost but the campaign he planned to do in order to launch her into success within the LA art community. It was a three-month-long project and would include many in-person events up and down the California coastline. David's heart twisted in a knot knowing if she went ahead with it, it'd mean extending her trip even longer. Finn's words at the end of the email were the final swing of the hammer driving the nails into hope's coffin. It read: ***You should've done all of this years ago, but at least you're starting now.***

Marking the email as *Unread,* David slid the phone back into her purse and returned to his seat across the table. David didn't know what to think, what to say, or how to feel about it. He glanced to the dance floor he and Cindy had just been on. Could he really put himself ahead of his wife's dreams of being an artist? No, not anymore, he couldn't. Soon, Cindy returned to the table.

As she sat down, she saw right through David. "You okay?"

"Your phone buzzed."

"Oh! I bet it was Finn. Let me check."

He watched Cindy carefully as she excitedly dug in her purse and pulled her phone out. David studied his wife as she unlocked the phone and read the email. Her countenance fell, and she put her phone back in her purse.

When a few moments went by without a word from her, he prompted her. "So?"

She shook her head, her eyes fixed on the glass of water in front of her. "It was him . . . But it's not going to happen."

While those were the exact words he thought he wanted to hear, he couldn't help but feel dissatisfied. "How come?"

"It's too much money and I just don't think it's the right time."

It was a lot of money, but the money was available and at her disposal. David was moved with compassion toward his wife and he recalled the end of the email from Finn. ***You should've done all of this years ago . . .*** David couldn't let his wife let go of her dreams because of the price or because of him. Reaching a hand across the table, he touched hers gently.

"Money isn't an issue. It's your dream, Cindy."

Frowning, she shook her head. "You haven't seen the price, David. It's too much."

Guilt for already knowing weighed heavily on his heart. "I have a confession. I looked at your phone and read the email. I *do* know the price. I'm saying do it."

"You saw the email? So, you saw the three months and the fact that I need to be in California longer?"

He nodded.

With that nod, Cindy's whole being lit up with joy and it ground his self-interest to powder instantly. She would be staying even longer in California now, and it was with his own approval and insistence. So why was his heart breaking at that thought?

THAT EVENING, Cindy stayed at David's hotel. After spending some time together in the room, David went for a walk after Cindy slipped off to slumber in the hotel room's bed. As he walked, he thought about not having his wife for an additional three months and it hurt. Though a part of David had hoped she'd fly home with him and cut the trip short after his arrival, he knew now that it'd not only not be cut short but instead extended.

Walking beneath the street lamps as he traveled on foot, he watched as cars zoomed by. Life was happening without him in California, and he would have to learn to be okay with that. Up until this point, the ability to press forward was fueled by the end being just a few more weeks or days away, but now it was months.

Finding a bench at a park a few blocks up from the hotel, David took a seat. Crossing his arms, he continued to watch the cars zip past him down the road. Closing his eyes, he bowed his head and prayed. *Have I already lost my wife? Did my screw ups last too long for our marriage to be redeemed and for her to want to be home with me? My heart is aching, my mind is spinning, and only You can see the future ahead of me. Please guide me, lead me, and strengthen me. Amen.*

David returned to the hotel and slipped into the bed with Cindy. As he slipped underneath the covers, he scooted close to his wife and wrapped his arms around her. David wasn't usually one for cuddling, but tonight would be an exception.

CHAPTER 22

SILENCE FILLED THE AIR BETWEEN Cindy and David over breakfast the next morning in the hotel restaurant. Cindy's time with her husband was dwindling down and tomorrow, he'd be flying back to Spokane while she stayed behind. They hadn't talked any more about Finn, the art, or the fact that she had decided to extend her stay for another three months. When David didn't get upset about her staying longer, she was a bit surprised. She thought he would've shut her down and blamed it all on the cost. He didn't act the way she thought he would, and she wanted to find out what was different.

"So, you seem different."

Wiping his mouth with his napkin, David peered up from his breakfast across the table at her. "How so?"

"Last night at the restaurant. The David I married and have known for a long time wouldn't have let it all go the way you did."

He nodded and then took another bite of food.

"What's going on with you? You seem different."

Finishing his bite, he set his fork down. Resting an arm

on the table, he held out a hand, palm up. "I'm trying to give you space, Cindy. Trying to love more like Jesus loves the church. I've done a terrible job of it for most of our marriage."

"It hasn't all been bad, David."

He shook his head. "You're wrong. My issue started long before anything went wrong in our marriage."

Cindy's heart warmed, noticing the fact that he'd avoided mentioning her past mistake. She raised her eyebrows, encouraging him to continue.

"My problem started when I was born. I was born with selfishness and sin in my heart. In our marriage, I have always acted in my own self-interest and never truly put you first."

"I feel like you used to put me first though."

Again, he shook his head. "Only because it benefited me in some way. I love you and I have always loved you, but it's always been about how you can benefit me. Through the last few weeks, God has been revealing more and more to me about myself." He paused, looking away for a moment, then his gaze came back to Cindy. "It's ugly and at times it hurts, but it's the truth and God is working in my heart through it."

"I don't know what to say . . ."

He shrugged and picked up his fork. "You don't have to say anything."

They continued eating, and as they did, Cindy thought about the distance between them that would be returning in another day. "I feel so nervous about your going back to Spokane."

"Why?"

"I don't know. I just miss you a lot, David. A part of me feels like I need to be home with you and working on our marriage. You know what they say, 'It's hard to work on a marriage when you're not home to work on it!' I just wonder if I'm being selfish and I need to just give this artist stuff up and come home."

Shaking his head, David reached a hand across the table and placed it atop Cindy's. His touch sent waves of electricity up her arm and across her whole body. Looking straight into her eyes, he said, "I love you and I want you to come home, but I want you to come home when you're ready to come home. Not a second sooner."

"But what about you?"

He shook his head, smiling as he withdrew his hand. "I'll be okay. God will help me."

THAT EVENING, the two of them joined Sarah for a Wednesday night service at the Calvary chapel church they had been attending since Cindy came to California. Cindy knew David enough to know that he didn't appreciate the modern worship service, so she leaned into his ear after the second song. "I know it's not what you're normally used to. I should've warned you."

He laughed lightly and turned toward her. "It's a bit modern . . . but hey, they're worshiping Jesus. That's the important thing."

The church they attended in Spokane was traditional in both their worship and routine of service. There were no electric guitars or drums but instead hymnals and an organ played by Mrs. Hammer every Sunday morning. Cindy was glad to see her husband open to other styles of worship. There was a time not long ago where David would've walked right out in frustration immediately after the band started. Smiling in that moment with David, Cindy took a step closer to him and looped her arm around his. They continued to sing praises to God together, band and all.

After worship finished, the pastor took to the stage while

a guitarist continued playing lightly. The pastor led a prayer that began with thankfulness for Jesus and ended with a blessing over the study of God's Word.

"Turn with me, if you would, in your Bible to Galatians chapter three."

The sound of pages turning filled the sanctuary's air.

"I love the sound of Bible pages turning! Hey, everyone, hold up your Bible for a moment."

Pausing, everyone in the sanctuary with a Bible, including Sarah, Cindy, and David, held up their Bibles.

"Isn't that beautiful? We're a Bible church! Praise the Lord!"

Praises to God and cheers erupted and then the congregation continued to turn in their Bibles to the third chapter of Galatians. The pastor then read.

You foolish Galatians! Who has bewitched you? Before your very eyes Jesus Christ was clearly portrayed as crucified. I would like to learn just one thing from you: Did you receive the Spirit by the works of the law, or by believing what you heard? Are you so foolish? After beginning by means of the Spirit, are you now trying to finish by means of the flesh? Have you experienced so much in vain—if it really was in vain? So again I ask, does God give you his Spirit and work miracles among you by the works of the law, or by your believing what you heard? So also Abraham "believed God, and it was credited to him as righteousness."

Galatians 3:1-6

"It's in our very nature to feel inclined to *earn* what we get. I'm sure you've all heard someone say, *'I don't need handouts!'* a time or two in your life. It reminds me of years ago when my wife and I were on welfare. That's right, we were on *food stamps*. I absolutely despised the fact that I had to use food stamps to buy food. On multiple occasions, I would, when I was alone at the store and there were people in line behind me watching, skip the food stamp card and instead use the cash in my wallet. Was it pride? Absolutely, it was. My prideful heart didn't want people seeing me use those food stamps, even though at the time, we needed them. You see, our prideful hearts don't want handouts. Most people want to *earn* everything that they get."

The pastor walked over to the pulpit and pressed a finger against his Bible. "Let's read this again. *'Did you receive the Spirit by the works of the law, or by believing what you heard?'* What the author, Paul, is doing here is helping the church recall how they got the Spirit to begin with. Our walk with Christ is a journey and we can and should end up serving and having a lot of fruits that come from walking with the Lord. But it's good to keep in mind and remember those works didn't save us. Those works came later and after we were saved. It was *faith* that saved us, church! Faith *alone*. The works are a byproduct of a transformed heart."

As Cindy continued to listen, she glanced over at David, who was busy taking notes on his little notebook he kept with his Bible. It warmed her heart to see her husband take such an interest in the things of God. He hadn't been that way for years.

After service let out, the three of them ventured into the fellowship hall for complimentary treats and coffee.

Grabbing a cookie with a napkin, Cindy turned to Sarah who was behind her in line.

"You going to miss this church after you move?"

She nodded. "But Pastor Niles told me about a good church in Simi Valley. It's an old friend of his from Seminary."

"That's cool!"

Sarah and Cindy walked over to the table where David was already sitting. He was deep in conversation with an older gentleman about the flaws of Calvinism.

The older man was speaking as Sarah and Cindy sat down near where David was standing. "The best way I've been able to wrap my head around a lot of this predestination stuff is to understand that God is outside of time. He is present in every single day of the history and future of the world. Also, he is present at the foundations of the world!"

"Yes." David smiled. "*And* being at both the foundations of the world and at the end of time, God is then able to see who will be saved. In a sense, they are predestined, but they still have the choice. 1 Timothy 2:4 tells us that God desires *all* to be saved, not some."

Cindy raised an eyebrow as she turned to her sister with a low voice. "Sounds like a pretty intense talk."

Sarah smiled and nodded. "Yes, it does. Hey, I didn't tell you, but Levi is moving to Chicago in two days."

"Oh, wow." Cindy took a sip of her coffee. "What's he doing that for?"

"He got some random job with a tech company."

"I didn't know he did anything with technology."

Sarah laughed. "Me either!"

"Well, that's good that he'll be moving."

"Yeah, I think so too. He said he sees it as a fresh start and a do-over at life."

"I hope he finds Jesus. That's the only thing that will ever change him."

"I know. That was my prayer for years . . ."

Reaching a hand over, Cindy lightly touched her sister's arm. "Don't ever stop praying for him."

"I won't."

Cindy's cellphone vibrated in her front pocket and she pulled it out to see that it was Melody.

"Hey, Mel! How are you?"

"Good. Is Dad still there with you?"

"Yes."

"Can I talk to him? He wasn't answering his phone."

Glancing over at David and seeing his conversation had just ended, she handed him the phone. He took the call a few feet away.

Sarah watched as he talked on the phone, then turned to Cindy.

"How is Melody doing?"

"Good. She sent me a picture of her belly this morning. It's getting pretty big. I think she and Tyson are really embracing their new life as a family in Concord."

Sarah nodded slowly. "I bet it's still hard being in a new town."

Cindy laughed and looked over at Sarah. "You're moving to a new town in two weeks!"

Joining in the laugh, her sister slapped Cindy's shoulder playfully.

THE NEXT MORNING, Cindy woke early with David at the hotel so she could take him to the airport. Her heart ached knowing in a short time, he'd be gone and she wouldn't see him for quite some time. As the clock wound down and it was almost time to head out, she stopped David on his way out of the bathroom in the hotel room. Resting a trembling hand on his chest, she peered into his eyes.

"I'm going to miss you."

He smiled and cupped her face in his warm hand. She leaned her cheek against his touch, never wanting it to stop.

"I'm going to miss you too."

"Should I just come home, David? Do I really need to stay? Is it silly to stay and pursue an art career at my age?"

"It's not silly. Remember what I said, love. Not a moment sooner."

Though her husband's words were full of support, she could sense in his eyes the exact heartache she felt in her soul. As they drove to the airport, the rising levels of discomfort pulled at the very breath in her lungs. She'd be losing David again, and this time it hurt far deeper. At least when she stormed out of that house to fly to California, she was angry. It wasn't so hard to deal with when she had the fuel of anger driving her. This, however, was just misery.

Standing outside the airport, she wrapped her arms tightly around David. They held each other tightly for a short few moments. She didn't want to ever let go of him. Cindy's heart didn't want him to get on that plane and fly away from her.

"Stay with me, David. Don't go!" Wiping her eyes, she shook her head as she pleaded with him.

His gaze lowered. "I have responsibilities I have to get back to."

"I know . . ." Cindy let out a defeated sigh.

Lifting his gaze to hers, he lifted her chin lightly with his index finger. "Just because I'm a thousand miles away doesn't mean I'm not right here with you."

He touched his finger against her chest where her heart was, and she melted. They kissed and exchanged goodbyes, and then he left.

CHAPTER 23

IT WASN'T UNTIL DAVID ARRIVED home that reality finally sank in. His life would have to go on without his wife for another three months. Shutting the front door behind him, he dropped his suitcase and stared into the dark and bleak future ahead. An ache crawled into his heart at that very moment and loneliness filled his entire being. Turning on the lights in the foyer, he proceeded deeper into his solitude. The pieces of mail he had placed on the kitchen counter were still in the exact place he left them. He had felt the sting of loneliness before he left, but now it somehow felt thicker, denser. Maybe it was because he had just spent three days with his wife. Maybe it was because he now knew he had another three months of waiting. He came to his recliner in the living room and kicked off his shoes. Plopping down, he reclined. He reached over to the lamp on the end table and switched it on. Relaxing back into his chair, he rested his hands behind his head and stared up at the lamp's light on the ceiling.

He thought of Cindy. It had been painful to see how much beauty was evident in her life away from him in California. Painful but at the same time insightful for him. How could he ever voice his desire for her to leave California behind when all that was waiting for her at home was him? Her husband, who had done nothing but treat her with contempt and distance for years. David's love for his wife was growing, and he had discovered in his time with her that he loved her too much to make her leave California before she was ready. He only wanted her to be happy now.

David rested in his recliner as he thought more about Cindy. She had seemed so happy and full of new life. Then a haunting and pervasive thought penetrated his mind. *What if she never wants to come back?* His eyes glistened knowing that it was a possibility.

His phone rang a few minutes later. It was Cindy.

"David?" Her voice was strained and filled with a heavy sorrow. He knew something was wrong.

He flung his feet down and jumped from his recliner. "What's wrong? You okay, Cindy?"

"It's my dad."

"Your dad?"

"Yes. He's in surgery right now. My sister just barely told me. They're trying to remove a tumor from his colon."

Sitting back down on the recliner, David smoothed a hand over his face. "Is it . . . cancer?"

"Yes."

"Oh, Cindy . . ."

"Can you please keep him in your prayers?"

"Yes. Are you going to fly out?"

"I called my mom and she insisted that I not. Kept saying none of it is a big deal." Cindy cried more, then sniffled. "I wish you were here with me right now."

David nodded. "Yeah, it would've been nice if your sister gave us a heads up before I flew out."

"She didn't know until this morning when my mom called her right before breakfast."

David's anger warmed inside him, but he prayed and pushed it away as soon as it started to rise. He couldn't let himself become enraged over the lack of communication on Cindy's parents' part. It wouldn't do any good. Taking a deep breath, he had an idea come to mind. "I'm flying back to California."

"David, please don't. I have my sister here and we'll get through it. Just pray, please?"

Hanging up with Cindy a few minutes later, David prayed for Hank and then afterward sat in his chair and stared into the dimly lit living room. His eyes caught the reflection of the lamp off the picture frame on the mantle. It was of Cindy and her parents when they were younger. He began to think about how Hank had wasted all these years on a grudge toward his daughter. The lost memories, the lost time with his grandchild, and why? Because he didn't like him. Smoothing his hands over his face, David dipped his chin and prayed. *God, help me to never be as blind as that man.*

After a little while passed, David got up and retrieved his Bible from his suitcase in the foyer. Taking his Bible into the kitchen, he sat down at the table and grabbed his notebook and pen from beside the napkin holder. He prayed again and asked for strength and direction in his life. Then he started reading in Ephesians, taking notes as he read each verse. As he ventured into chapter four, he realized he was reading a set of instructions, so his notes detailed the instructions he discovered for Christian living and adapted them into his own life.

1. No longer have futility (or pointlessness) in my thinking (Ephesians 4:17-19)

2. Put off my old self (my self-focused tendencies) (Ephesians 4:22-23)

3. Speak truthfully from my lips (Never lie, not even in small matters. Also speak the truth always, never stay silent.) (Ephesians 4:25)

4. Do not sin in my anger (Keep the lips shut when heated) (Ephesians 4:26-27)

5. Do not steal, but instead work (Stay purposeful in all that is done and do it unto the Lord) (Ephesians 4:28)

6. Speak from my lips only what is helpful in building up, not tearing down (No ill-will is to come out of my mouth) (Ephesians 4:29)

7. Do not grieve the Holy Spirit within me (Don't go against the commands of God or His nature) (Ephesians 4:30)

8. Rid myself of bitterness, rage, anger, brawling, slander, malice (Stop focusing on what hurts me and start focusing on others and God only) (Ephesians 4:31)

9. Be kind, compassionate, forgiving (Love like Jesus so I can live like Jesus) (Ephesians 4:32)

AFTER WRITING THE NOTES, David read them over again and prayed over each instruction and asked the Lord for His divine help. As he studied more of God's Word and directed all his thoughts on Christ and others, David was filled with a supernatural peace. After he finished his time in the Scriptures, he called his friend Tyler.

"Hey, David. You back in town?"

"Yes. Just got back a few hours ago. Are the guys getting together tonight for Bible study?"

A snap of a board sounded in the background, startling David. "Sorry about that, David. One of the guys here with me at this old hotel is trying to break down some boards on a window. No group tonight."

"An old hotel?"

"Yes, remember that second-chance home I was talking about before you left?"

"Oh, yeah." David laughed. "That was only three days ago. You already found a place?"

"Yes! It turned out a client of Jonathan's and mine had an unused motel from the eighties and he said we could use it if we fixed it up and he'd lease it cheaply. The only catch was we had to move quickly because he had an interested buyer. So now I'm down here, getting my hands dirty. I couldn't help but start right away on it."

Tyler's excitement was contagious. "Would you like a hand?"

"Oh, you don't have to do that, David."

"No, I'd love to help! The physical labor would be a welcome feeling at this time."

"All right. I'll text you the address."

Hanging up with Tyler, David got in his car and drove down to the hotel. The condition of the property was poor, but with a bit of imagination, David could see the potential as he pulled into the parking lot. Finding a work truck loaded with garbage and wood scraps parked outside one of the rooms with a light on, David parked beside it and went inside. Stepping over a hole in the floor, he maneuvered carefully past a busted and mangled spring bed. He found Tyler in the bathroom with a layer of sweat on his forehead and covered in filth.

Out of breath, Tyler stood up from the bathtub and stepped out of the tub.

David embraced him in a brotherly hug.

"My buddy Vinny just left. This place is a dive!"

Glancing around the bathroom at the peeling paint and grime, David nodded in agreement. His gaze fell back on

Tyler. "It will take some time, but I can see it coming together."

Tyler grinned. "Yeah? I'm not delusional?"

"Not at all, and it's a noble task." David clapped his hands together and peered around at the work that needed to be done. "Tell me what you want me to do."

"First, go to my truck and grab the work gloves off the bench. Then you can go grab that mattress and box spring and get them into the bed of the truck. Then go next door and start gutting the furniture out of it. I'm going to keep work on checking the walls for mold and rotten beams."

"You got it, Captain!"

Leaving the bathroom, David went out to the truck and grabbed the work gloves. It wasn't what David envisioned for the rest of his day, but it was enjoyable to spend time working with his hands and with his brother in Christ. The labor was intensive and filthy, but knowing it would serve in reaching people for Jesus was enough for him.

THE NEXT MORNING, with aching muscles and a sore back, David arrived into his office and promptly sat down in his chair. Taking a deep breath, he prayed and then scooted closer to his desk. He powered on his PC and took a drink of his coffee. As he logged into his email, a knock sounded on the door.

"Come in."

Mark entered his office, along with a man he didn't recognize.

"David, this will be your new business partner, Albert Roy."

A sense of being caught off guard overwhelmed David and he leapt up from his chair. Coming around his desk, he shook hands with Albert.

"It's nice to meet you, Albert."

"You too. Do you mind if we sit and chat for a bit?"

"Sure. But can I talk to Mark for a moment?"

"Yes, my cup of coffee needs a refill anyway." Albert left the office and David shut the door behind him. He whipped around to face Mark.

"What are you doing? I didn't even get a chance to get back to you on whether I wanted to sell my portion."

Mark shrugged. "I assumed when you left for California and said nothing in your text about wanting to sell, you decided not to sell. Did you want to sell?"

"No." David furrowed his eyebrows.

"Then what's the problem?"

"The problem is you just bring this guy into my office and you tell me he is my new business partner! These kinds of things take time and paperwork."

Mark laughed. "Well, excuse me for trying to move quickly on this. The paperwork is in the works. You know me enough to know I don't like waiting around."

"That's true." David's nerves started to calm down. He saw Albert outside his office window. Sighing, David shook his head and looked at Mark again. "Whatever. I'll meet with him. Make sure you have Legal get the documents and everything in place."

"They're already working on it." Patting David's shoulder, Mark smiled at him. "Just relax, David."

Mark left, and Albert walked into the office. Returning to behind his desk, David sat down.

"I know this is all weird right now for you, David. But rest assured, these wrinkles all over my face and body are stamps of experience."

Laughing, David nodded. "Have a seat, Albert."

Albert and David began to talk. They talked management styles of the team in place, business practices, and even holiday pay for employees. Then Albert took the conversation into what he saw for the future for *Carlton's*. After two and a half hours of being talked at, David held up a hand.

"Albert. Listen, I'm glad we got a chance to sit down, but I can't agree with a lot of what you're saying here."

He adjusted in his seat and nodded, sighing with what seemed to be disappointment. "Ah. I see. You don't like me, do you?"

"No, it's not that. We've just been doing things a certain way for so long and you're talking an awful lot about change."

"I see. Well, growth requires change, David."

"We're the largest in the area!" David laughed and held out his hands. "What more do you want?"

"I want global domination." Albert chuckled lightly and then proceeded. "You and Mark have done great with the company thus far, but the growth has stalled from what I saw in the preliminary reports. I want to take it to the next level and expand upward and outward. That's going to take change on every level of the company."

"A lot of these people working here have been here for years. I know them, and they won't like all of this change."

"I'm sure they won't mind their paychecks changing in an upward direction." He laughed. "That's change they can all embrace! You see, at the end of the day, David, I'm a family man. I want to take care of my employees who are taking care of my customers."

"I'm glad to hear you say that." David smiled as his heart warmed. Families and his people were what he cared about too. It was nice to hear Albert at least care about the employees.

"Look, David. I'm a good guy, not the enemy. I'm excited to be a part of *Carlton's* and I'm also excited for the future.

I've been in the wholesale business for over forty years now and I know how to take this business to the next level."

Albert's expertise and words would've made the old David full of excitement as he looked toward the future. But instead, it made him think about all the extra work he'd be putting in as a result. He nodded at Albert as he continued about the bright future ahead and how much money they'd both make. Something deep inside him felt a resistance toward Albert, toward the future of himself at Carlton's. Was this the beginning of the end?

CHAPTER 24

PRAYING FOR HER FATHER WHO refused to have anything to do with her was both frustrating and revealing in nature. It frustrated her that he was blinded by stubbornness and bound to a life sentence of never knowing his grandchild or great-grandchildren. Her prayers were revealing to Cindy because they shone a light on the forgiveness she refused to give the man. He had hurt her deeply by his refusal to acknowledge David as her husband and walk her down the aisle. She still harbored animosity toward him for that, and though she didn't want him to die in surgery, she couldn't help but feel he had it all coming to him.

"What's wrong, Sarah?" Cindy's question came as Sarah was sitting on the couch the morning after their father's surgery.

"Nothing." Sarah's eyes didn't connect with Cindy's but instead stayed fixed on the California downpour out the window.

"I don't believe you." Cindy stopped in front of her in the

living room and rested a hand on her hip. "I'm not leaving this room until you tell me."

Sarah's red eyes turned to Cindy softly. "You said some mean stuff about Dad yesterday. It was *really* hateful."

"Well, he has said some pretty unkind stuff to me and about me too!"

Shaking her head, Sarah shrugged. "So? You get a free pass because he does it?"

Her sister's words cut through the layers of pride in Cindy's heart, causing her to pause. Moving over to the couch where Sarah was sitting, Cindy took a seat. Her shoulders slumped.

Sitting upright beside Cindy, Sarah rested a hand on her back. "Dad's a jerk, but he's still your dad."

Eyes welling with tears as her heart splintered, Cindy turned to her. "I know that, but I don't want to let him back into my heart."

"Forgiveness isn't about you and him. It's not giving him permission to hurt you again. It's not saying what has happened is okay. It's about you and God, Sis."

Cindy's heart returned to hardness as memories of her father's words filtered through her heart. "I can't."

Standing up, she left the room.

THREE WEEKS after her father's surgery and David's return to Spokane, Cindy found herself missing home more than ever. Though she and David spoke on the phone daily, it never felt as if it was enough. Cindy missed her husband's touch, his scent, and most of all, just the feeling of him being near her. Four days ago, Finn informed Cindy that the weekend's art exhibit they had scheduled was canceled, so she immediately booked a flight home for November fifth, two days from now.

Today was moving day for herself and Sarah. They were leaving the giant mansion in LA and moving into a small apartment in Simi Valley. It wouldn't be as big as Sarah's old residence, but it'd be *hers*.

After the group of teenagers from the new church left the apartment that afternoon, Sarah promptly fell into the couch cushions on the sofa.

"*Finally!* Peace and relaxation." Sarah smiled as her gaze caught Cindy's.

The corner of Cindy's lips curled into a smile as she walked over and sat down on the couch. "Nice to be out on your own now?"

"Absolutely. Now to unpack this place before I start my job on Monday. What time are you meeting Finn tomorrow?"

"One o'clock. He said the last three weeks have been going good for the audience building he has been doing online for me. Plus, those art shows we've been doing have been getting good press. Lots of stuff happening."

"That's good." Sarah smiled as she sat upright on the couch and she held out her hands as if Cindy was a trophy. "My sister, Cindy Carlton, a known LA artist."

They both laughed and then Cindy shook her head and stood up.

"I'm going to go call David."

Sarah raised her eyebrows. "Tell *Romeo* hello for me."

Cindy smiled back at her sister, then proceeded out onto the patio off the kitchen. When David answered on the other end of the line, her heart dipped into her stomach. Just hearing his voice was torture to her these days. The anticipation was driving the two of their hearts wild.

"Two more days!" She smiled as she spoke and glanced at the towering palm trees a few feet from the patio.

"I don't think I'll make it two more days." They both

laughed lightly, then he promptly changed the subject. "How'd the move go?"

"Ten boys showed up last night to pack the U-Haul and then five this afternoon to unpack it. Sarah and I barely had to move boxes!"

"Oh, wow! That is awesome."

"Right? She is apparently exhausted from those boxes though." Cindy turned and peered in through the sliding glass door at her sister on the couch. "Oh, I got a text from Finn. I have a meeting with him tomorrow at one. He said there is a surprise for me that I'll be happy about."

"A surprise?"

"Yes, I don't know what it means, but I think it's a good thing. I'll let you know what happens."

"Please do."

Cindy continued to chat with David for a short while more, talking about Melody and her new baby about to enter the world in two months. David then spoke about the changes happening at work. She prayed for her husband's work life every night before she went to bed, but she felt his heart was losing passion for the job every time he talked about it.

"I can't wait to hold you in my arms again, Cindy."

"Mmm. It's going to be perfect."

THE FOLLOWING DAY, at one o'clock, Cindy sat down at a table with Finn at a café in LA. Instead of his laptop this time, he had a large folder and in it were papers. As he pulled each paper out that contained various data points, he detailed to Cindy how the progression thus far in the campaign for launching her artist name had been successful. At the end of all the data points, he closed the folder and looked squarely into her eyes.

"Okay. You know how we've done a couple of exhibits and they have been okay?"

She nodded.

"Okay. Ready for the surprise?"

Her eyes grew as she nodded.

"You know how we had that cancellation for tomorrow?"

"Yes." She grew nervous, wondering why he was talking about tomorrow, the day she was flying out to Spokane.

"I was able to get you booked at an art show at Huntington Beach instead! Vasco Esiel will be there!"

Her insides jumped at hearing the name *Vasco*. He was a well-respected artist not only locally, but on a national scale. Finn had bragged about Vasco being one of his clients in the past, and the fact he had come back to do an art show and she was invited was tremendous news. Cindy knew not only would he and his fans be in attendance, but gobs of media also. This was a chance to break out big. There was only one problem. She wouldn't be seeing David tomorrow if she did the art show.

"*Oh . . .*" Her heart crumbled as she thought of David.

"Oh?" Finn scoffed and shook his head. "That's strange. I thought you would be a little bit happier to have your art sitting next to the likes of Vasco Esiel!"

"I am. That's great." Pushing aside her sadness, she tried to stay focused. Cindy forced out a grin. "I'm excited!"

After meeting with Finn that afternoon, Cindy took a drive down to the beach and went out onto a pier. She needed time to process, time to think before she called David to discuss. As she strolled across the planks of wood on the pier, she couldn't help but notice all the couples around her. Young and old and all different sizes. Each couple held onto each other like they never wanted to let go. *I never wanted to let go of him.* She missed David more now than ever. In her heart, Cindy already knew he'd be understanding about postponing the trip. He had grown more understanding and caring in the time they had been apart than during all their years of marriage. It annoyed her at the same time it made her feel more loved. She missed him terribly, loved him beyond her own understanding, and wanted nothing more than to be with him once again. But her art. She needed to finish the work and go home the right way.

After spending a couple of hours on the pier, staring out into the vast and wide expanse of the ocean, Cindy left and headed back toward her car. As she walked, she pulled her phone out and called David.

"Really?" David was discontented with hearing about the art showing at the beach. Then, he recovered and his tone shifted. "Well . . . if you need to do this, you should do it."

His kindness sparked a wildfire of sudden and explosive anger in her.

"Why can't you fight for me, David? Act like you *need* me the way I feel I need you."

He was quiet for a long moment. Then when he finally spoke, he spoke with confidence and absolution in his voice. "I love you and want you, Cindy, but I only *need* the Lord."

Quietness filled the next moment. She was caught off-guard by the comment. "You don't need me?"

"You are my helpmate and I love you dearly, more than any human being on this planet, but I have learned I *can* live without you. Though I do not prefer this, I can do it. I can go days, weeks, and even months without you. My God? My Savior? My Creator? I can't go a single moment without Him. He holds the very breath in my lungs. He holds my entire being together. This time apart from you has been difficult and trying on my soul. But *Cindy* . . . through it, God has been teaching me a particularly important fact. He has been showing me that it's He whom I need to rely on, not you. This problem runs deep and explains a lot from all those years ago when you made that mistake. I was so heavily reliant on you that I couldn't take your trespass. I closed down and pushed everything and everyone away . . . including God. It was idolatry the way I held you up in my heart, the way I held you up in my mind. But that is no more. God is my only number one."

A portion of Cindy wanted to be upset, but she knew she couldn't. In seconds, her attitude shifted from one of anger to one of longing. She longed to have a reliance on God the way David appeared to now possess. After processing his words a moment longer as she got into the car, she buckled her seatbelt and then peered out her windshield at the ocean. She smiled.

"How do you take something painful and make it beautiful?"

"What do you mean?"

"Like the pain of being away from your spouse and turn it into something beautiful about how it's brought you closer to God?"

"Oh, honey, I didn't do a thing. That's all God and His glory. You can attest to the fact of how rotten a person I can be from what you witnessed these last ten years. You've seen me at my absolute worst. Though I am learning more and have made some changes, I know I am still a selfish and stupid man. With that being said, anything beautiful or good you see in me is not me at all. It's God, and God alone."

Cindy's heart grew deeper in love with her husband in that moment. He was becoming more than the man she had longed for him to be, a man truly dedicated to God. Lifting a prayer of thankfulness up toward Heaven, she thanked God with tears in her eyes.

CHAPTER 25

HANGING UP THE PHONE CALL after finding out Cindy wasn't coming for the visit, David fell to his knees in his living room. Hands clasped together and tears running down his cheeks, he pressed into prayer with God. The strength of God's Spirit he felt moments ago while on the phone call had faded immediately after hanging up. He knew there were still strands of dependence on his wife within him, and he sought after God for comfort and peace of mind. Coupled with the rising tensions at work, David knew his faith was being put to the test.

He prayed aloud. "God, I don't get it. My business is turning into something I don't want, my wife is choosing work over me, and my daughter is thousands of miles away. I feel like I'm being dragged out to a desert to be killed. It's like the more I press into You, God, the more difficult my life becomes. Please help me. Please strengthen my spirit within me. Please help me understand this trying time in my life!"

As his lips uttered his prayerful confession, he instantly was taken back to his Bible reading a few mornings ago. *Meshach, Shadrach, and Abednego.* David picked himself up from the floor and sat down on the couch and grabbed his Bible from the coffee table. Opening to Daniel 3, he skimmed as he prayed and asked God in his mind, *what is it?* Then, he stopped on verse 25, a chill falling over him as he did.

He said, "Look! I see four men walking around in the fire, unbound

and unharmed, and the fourth looks like a son of the gods."

Daniel 3:25

Jesus. Jesus was in the furnace with the three men. The gears in David's mind pieced it together. *He didn't stop the men from being tossed into the furnace, but instead He was with them in the fire.* David's heavy heart was replaced with a joy-filled one as he applied the principal of the Scripture to his own life. *God won't stop the pain from coming, but He will be with me during it.* God was with David, and he only truly realized it in that moment. More tears came rolling down his cheeks. This time, the tears were from the joyfulness in David's heart from hearing God's voice through His Word. David was comforted in his affliction.

Meeting for Bible study a few hours later, David greeted everyone with a curt wave as he entered the living room a few minutes late and sat down. Everyone went around in the circle and shared how their week had been going. Jonathan talked about his and Tyler's design business suffering the loss of a special client and dear friend, Ann Ellison, and Tyler spoke about the progress of the second-chance shelter he was working on during free time. Charlie spoke of his daughter's amazing progress in school, and then it finally came to David.

David was quiet for a moment as his mind thumbed through the rolodex of latest happenings at work and life. There was good and there was bad, but he couldn't pick what to talk about, so he laughed lightly and shook his head as he smiled.

"What can I say? God is good."

"Yes, but what's going on?" Charlie asked. "You have the Mrs. coming home for a visit tomorrow, right?" Charlie hadn't known about the canceled trip. Not even Tyler knew about it.

"That got canned."

Heads hung around the circle. They all knew how precious her trip was to David.

"Oh, man. How come?" Jonathan inquired as he leaned slightly forward in his chair.

"Some art show on a beach with a guy who wears fancy hats. Man, I don't know. It doesn't really matter. God's really utilizing this time to do some pruning and I just have to be patient."

"That's your wife," Tyler responded. He pointed toward the front door. "She's your wife! You can't just let this keep going on. You're only allowing this from guilt of your past mistakes with her."

A lesser man would've been offended by Tyler's words, but David was not. "You have a valid point there, but the reality is that we can't control people. I can't control her. And why would I want to? It's her life and she's got to make decisions for herself. I can't hold her hand and point everything out that she should and should not do. It's kind of like God and us. He's a perfect gentleman. He doesn't force us to do what He wants. He gives us freedom and in that freedom is where true love resides." David paused, realizing his own words. Then he continued. "Believe me, I've tried to control her. It didn't do anyone any good. And now . . . And now God is showing me how to truly rely on Him, which is far better and superior than relying on Cindy or any flawed person."

Charlie chimed in. "There isn't anything in the Bible about it being okay or not okay to spend time apart like what's going on here with you and Cindy. It's kind of a unique situation. Granted, I would say we reap what we sow, and you've got to be careful with all this time apart."

"That's good to remember. Thank you, Charlie." David hadn't thought about that aspect of the time apart from Cindy. He had only thought about the benefits in his relationship to God and how he was growing in his dedication and affection for the Lord. As the Bible study continued over the next hour, he thought back to Charlie's comment several times throughout. As everyone filed out the door to go home at the close of the evening, David was the last one to collect his belongings.

"How are you handling things?" Charlie's question came in a more intimate moment as everyone had left.

David put his coat on and then grabbed his Bible from his chair. He turned to Charlie and let out a sigh. "It's hard, but I'm getting through it. I'm more worried about the transitions at work, honestly."

"Oh, that's right. You have a new business partner, right? How's that going?"

"Not good. He's recreating systems, restructuring schedules, and implementing new policies. I have to punch a clock now and log hours. It's just . . . different."

"You mentioned before that you still have the option to sell your portion to him. Have you thought anymore about that?"

"Yes, a little. I'm not sure about doing that though. Some

part of me would love to retire, but then what? A scary thought to dwell on right now."

Charlie nodded and patted David's shoulder. "Pray about it and let the Lord lead you."

"I will. Thanks for opening your inn up to our little weekly get-togethers. You and the guys have been a blessing to my life in a such a big way."

Smiling, Charlie said, "It's been my pleasure."

TWO MONTHS CAME and went with little change. Cindy had informed David that her dad was out of the hospital and was given a clean bill of health. And David now was finding a new normal routine in life back in Spokane without his wife. He didn't like living without her, but he endured it nonetheless. His daughter, Melody, was due to give birth in a week, and he'd be flying out on Saturday to visit and be there for the birth. Leaving work early one Tuesday afternoon for a doctor's appointment, David took the rest of the day off so he could avoid Albert. It was the first time he took a half-day off work in over twenty-four years of business, excluding holidays. Honestly, David was growing tired of Albert's constant latest ideas to take things to the next level.

David left his doctor's office after getting a clean bill of health and headed over to the renovation site of Tyler's shelter. He hadn't seen him at the men's group the last two weeks and wanted to see if there was anything he could help with after hearing Jonathan mention last Thursday that Tyler was struggling. He also simply missed his friend. When David arrived onsite, he found the frozen January parking lot empty of the usual work trucks and only spotted Tyler's truck parked outside the hotel office. Something seemed wrong immediately. David promptly parked beside the truck and headed for the office door.

Walking through the doorway, he spotted Tyler standing on a ladder, painting the wall.

"How's it going?"

Tyler glanced over at David and when his gaze connected with David's, he broke into a smile and pulled out his ear buds.

"Hello, brother!"

David approached around the counter, smiling as Tyler came down the steps of the ladder.

They hugged and patted each other's backs.

"Need a hand around here, kid?"

Tyler shrugged as his gaze went out the office windows. "You probably noticed all the workers are gone, eh?"

"I did. Why is that?"

"Funding ran out, man. We had an investor back out. Now it's up to me to finish the painting and hope I can find a new investor to get operations going. I've already exhausted all my own resources and even some of Jonathan's that he has graciously donated, and it has just been way more money than we originally figured. We both gave up our savings for this, and if it ends up being for nothing, I don't know how I'll be able to face Jonathan or my wife after this."

"Wow that's rough, Brother! It's hard to count the costs of the unexpected like that mold situation last month that you ran into."

"Right? It makes me think with all this resistance, maybe it's not God's will." Tyler looked worried.

"If anything, it's the devil trying to keep you from doing good. Tell me what you need me to do and I'll do it."

He pointed out the window. "If you go down to unit 24, there are some paint supplies and paint suits. Start on room 25 and just start painting until you're done wanting to paint."

David set to work right away. As he started in on painting a short while later, he was filled with a sense of purpose and direction, just like he had experienced each time he came and helped. It was something that had been lacking in his work life since Albert became a partner. An idea suddenly came to David's mind as he changed the wall's color with a stroke of his paintbrush from an ugly yellow to an eggshell white. *What if I sell and invest it into this shelter?* The idea was one that not long ago, he'd never entertain, but right now, it didn't sound like such a horrible idea. As the idea swirled in his thoughts, his anxiety levels rose like flood waters in a home. He didn't want to let go. Pushing the idea away, David focused on painting over the yellow wall and let the idea fade from his mind.

CHAPTER 26

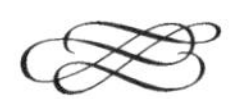

VASCO ESIEL HAD FALLEN IN love with Cindy's artwork two months ago at Huntington Beach and asked her to join him on an exclusive tour up and down the California coast. The tour would last for the remainder of her time in California. They were at their second-to-last showing in the city of San Francisco in early January when Cindy had to excuse herself to use the ladies' room. As she came out of the stall and set her purse on the counter, she peered at herself in the mirror. She looked great in the black cocktail dress she was wearing, or at least that's what David had told her when she sent him a picture of herself from the hotel room earlier that evening. *I can't wait to see him,* she thought to herself as she washed her hands and thought about Melody's due date next week. She dried her hands off on a towel when her cellphone rang. Pulling her phone out from her purse, she saw it was Melody. Her heart dipped.

"You okay, Mel?"

"I'm on the way to the hospital!"

Glancing toward the restrooms' doorway leading out to

the gallery, she shook her head as excitement and adrenaline started to course through her. "You sure it's not another Braxton Hicks?"

"Yes. I can tell this is really it!" Pausing for a contraction on the other end of the phone, her daughter was unable to speak and let out a pained groan.

Cindy had hoped to finish the art tour and fly out next Tuesday. Babies had a way of not caring about what people planned, though, and Cindy knew that. *I should've just left this week,* she thought with a guilty conscience as she remembered last week's conversation within herself on leaving early. It didn't matter now. She had to leave.

If she hurried to the airport and caught the next flight out, she might make it in time for the birth. That was only if Melody was in labor as long as she was with Alice. She could quite possibly miss the entire thing regardless of how quickly she made it to Concord. She touched her forehead as stress weighed in on her in the moment. There were no guarantees in this situation outside of the fact that Finn and Vasco would be offended at her departure.

Collecting her thoughts, Cindy refocused.

"I'm heading to the airport now, Mel."

"You don't have to do that."

"Oh, hush. Have Tyson text me the name and address of the hospital so I can give it to the cab driver."

"Okay. Mom?"

"Yes?"

"Thank you."

As she hung up with her daughter, Cindy paused as she caught her reflection in the mirror of the ladies' restroom. She could see her nervousness written all over her face. To tell Finn and Vasco the news wouldn't be easy. Suddenly, she remembered David. *I have to call him.* Dialing his number, she waited for him to answer.

"She's in labor, David."

"What? Now?" David inquired. "That's inconvenient for you. I know you're all dressed up at the function right now."

"My daughter isn't an inconvenience. I'm her mother. You flying out tonight or tomorrow?"

He didn't say anything for a long moment, then he cleared his throat. "I actually can't go right now."

Shaking her head as surprise lit in her tone, Cindy inquired further. "Why?"

"Albert is rolling out our revamped website tomorrow to the team, and I have to be here for it. I will come as soon as I can after it."

"*Oh.* I should've assumed it was work-related." The cut in her tone was filled with animosity over more than just missing this special event. It carried with it all the missed school plays, church potlucks, and a list of other events from the past that David had missed all in the name of *work*. David couldn't even make it to his first grand daughter's birth in the same city because of a 'work emergency.' Now he was missing this too. Cindy's anger warmed, feeling a sense that all the change she had seen in him had been a lie.

"Don't be like that, Cindy."

"No, David. You don't be like that. Your true colors are shining through right now. You honestly had me going for months. I thought you were a changed man, *David*. The truth of the matter is you were putting on a show the whole time."

He was quiet on the other end of the phone. It was long enough to make Cindy uneasy.

Finally, she spoke again. "Aren't you going to say something?"

David let out a heavy sigh. "What is there to say? You're my wife but it's like we live completely different lives. You want to spit vile and destructive comments to only tear me down right now. I understand your frustration right now in this moment, but to say everything is a show I've been putting on is an outright lie and hurtful. I have moved on from the past, and I think it's best that you learn how to do that too."

Cindy shook her head. "I have to go, David."

Hanging up with David, she cleared her mind and focused on the task ahead—telling Finn and Vasco she was abruptly leaving to fly out. Walking out of the bathroom, she purposely held her chin high in the attempt to make herself feel a measure more confident than she was feeling at the moment. Walking up to Finn, she tapped him on the shoulder, and he turned from the well-dressed couple he was speaking to at the moment.

"What is it?" His voice was hushed and laced with annoyance.

"I'm leaving."

"What?"

"I'm flying out for the birth of my grandbaby in New Hampshire."

"No, you're not. You have an obligation to follow through for the next few days. You can spend forever with your grandchild after this week is over, for all I care. But you are *not* leaving."

Anxiety rose within her as she saw Vasco walking toward the two of them. She turned her attention back to Finn.

"*Actually*, I am leaving."

She turned to leave, but he wrapped his hand around her arm and stopped her. Vasco arrived a moment later.

"What is going on here?" Vasco inquired as a look of confusion scattered across his face. He looked at Cindy and then at Finn.

Cindy yanked her arm away from Finn. "I have to leave to New Hampshire. I have a grandbaby coming into the world tonight."

Vasco's face softened, and he opened his arms as he came closer and hugged her. "Congratulations, Cindy! We might make beautiful paintings, you and I, but the most beautiful work of art is that of life by our Creator's hand!"

Her heart warmed at hearing Vasco speak of God for the first time in the months they had spent together on tour. Judging by the look on Finn's face, he was surprised by the comment as well. Finn's anger settled at Vasco's approval of her leaving, but it was evident Finn was still irritated by the departure. After exchanging goodbyes, Cindy worked her way through the crowd toward the exit. Stepping out onto the art gallery's steps, she was stopped once more by Finn.

"Don't ever come back to me. You're done as my client."

It wasn't surprise at what he had said to Cindy. With her eyes still fixed on Finn, it was only then that she realized it never mattered if her art had success or if she had fame. What mattered most to her was the relationships in her life and the people she loved. If only she had realized that sooner in life. Without a word, she turned away from Finn and continued down the steps to the curb, then she hailed for a cab to the airport.

ARRIVING at the Hospital in Concord, New Hampshire, Cindy made her way to the delivery floor of the hospital and spoke with the ladies at the desk about the room Melody was in. Strolling through the hospital room's doorway just shy of midnight, Cindy came into the dimly lit room. Still in her black cocktail dress she had worn to the gala, she looked upon her sleeping daughter and her husband. She smiled as tears welled in her eyes. Cindy had missed the birth. Her heart ached knowing she hadn't been there. Slipping out from sleep, Tyson blinked his eyes open and stood from the recliner he was resting in.

He came closer to Cindy and with a hushed voice spoke softly to her. "Come with me to the nursery and I'll introduce you to Jack."

"Aww. A boy! Congrats!"

He smiled and nodded, then led the way down the hallway toward the nursery. As they walked, she inquired about the birth.

"I am surprised she's asleep."

"She had a lot of pain and the medicine zonked her out an hour after she gave birth."

Cindy's heart flinched. *I should've been here.* The guilt of her decisions with Finn and pursuing her career as an artist weighed heavily on her heart. It was as if a light bulb had come on in her mind and she was suddenly aware of how selfish she had been throughout the entire thing. Not only had she missed the birth of Jack, but she had neglected the very man whom she loved. What started as a trip to help her sister during a time of crisis had turned into an extended time away from her husband. And it all was in the pursuit of her own selfish desires. Yet through it all, David had been patient with her. Cindy's heart ached but at the same time warmed, realizing how much David loved her. He had been selfless while she had been selfish. *I have to make things right with David,* she thought as they came to the nursery wing of the hospital. *But can he forgive me? Will he forgive me? Have I pushed him away too far?*

As they arrived at the nursery doorway, Tyson turned to her.

"Melody told Jack shortly after holding him for the first time that you were on your way to meet him. She was really happy about your coming. Thank you."

Even though she hadn't been there for the birth, her daughter was still happy about her coming. It made her feel loved even more and her eyes glistened with tears. "I'm so glad I'm here tonight."

He smiled and the two of them walked into the nursery. Traveling through a row of babies, they came to a basket and stopped.

"There he is." Tyson pointed to a baby.

Cindy's heart melted as she lifted little Jack up into her arms. Holding that little baby close to her, she peered down at the new life and was filled with awe, with wonder. Just then, she recalled Vasco's words earlier and she prayed, *God, you truly are the greatest Artist.*

CHAPTER 27

SLEEP DIDN'T COME EASILY FOR David that night. He tossed and turned and thought about Cindy and her words earlier on the phone. He wasn't putting on a show. David knew he was a different person than he used to be, but deep down, he knew he was still holding onto *Carlton's* as part of who he was. He didn't even like work the way he used to. His new business partner, Albert, annoyed him, and he dreaded each morning he had to go in, but he stayed with it. He kept going in day after day, perhaps because it was the only thing that was consistent in his life for the last couple of decades.

Giving up the fight to sleep, David sat up in his bed with a jerk. Raking a hand through his hair, he bowed his head and prayed. *God, I know You are already in tomorrow and You can see everything when I see very little. Please help me understand what I need to do. I'm scared, and I don't know what Your will is in my life.*

Pausing his prayer, he glanced over at the nightstand at the glaring red numbers that read *4:04 AM*. His insides ached with a longing for sleep. He hadn't slept more than a few hours all night.

He soon left the bedroom and walked down the hall. Pausing at the wedding photo of Melody and Tyson, he recalled his promise to her before she moved. *I'll be there.* Knowing he had broken his promise to Melody only drove the pain of the situation deeper into his heart.

Journeying into the kitchen, he put on a pot of coffee and sat down at the kitchen table. Immediately, he grabbed his Bible from across the table and pulled it close to him. His time with God was like oxygen to David these days. He opened up the Scriptures to continue his reading from last night.

Later that morning, when he was heading out the door to work, his cellphone rang. It was Cindy. Stopping halfway out the door, he answered the call.

"Hey." Her voice was soft, much gentler than their last conversation.

"So? Did you meet my grandson? I saw the pictures come through from Tyson late last night."

"I did . . ."

David could tell she was holding something back. "What's on your mind? You seem conflicted."

"I am. I'm sorry."

"I forgive you. I'm sure you had a lot on your mind to deal with last night. I'm sure it wasn't easy."

"I mean for *everything*, David."

David's eyes welled with tears as his heart knew before his mind what she meant. "I love you, Cindy."

"I love you too."

Continuing outside, he shut the door behind him and walked through the snow out to his car. "How's the new mom holding up?"

"Good. She was sleeping when I got here last night. Tyson

said she was heavily medicated for pain and passed out after the delivery. She hasn't woken up yet today."

"Hopefully, she is okay."

"She will be. She has her momma now. Sarah texted me this morning. I guess they found more cancer in Dad."

David's heart dipped. "Really? I thought your dad had a clean bill of health after that surgery a couple of months back."

Quiet for a moment, she sniffled, then responded. "I did too. But I guess he was having some issues and went in again. The cancer has spread."

"So, chemo?"

Her voice quieted. "*No.*" Hearing his wife's voice break and a soft sob sound on the other end of the phone broke David's heart. Then she said, "He's being moved into hospice."

David looked out the windshield at his house and blinked a few times. "Wow."

"*Yeah.*" Cindy cleared her throat and her voice picked up volume. "But I'm trying to not think about that right now. Right now is about Melody and her precious new baby boy. I want to focus on that."

Swallowing, David nodded and wiped the tears away from his eyes. "Okay."

"I'd better get back to the room and see if she's up yet. Have a good day at work, David."

"Thank you. I'll be praying for you. Give my grandson some extra loving from his grandpa."

Hanging up with Cindy, David took an extra few minutes to pray that morning as his car warmed up in the driveway. He prayed for comfort to wrap around his wife, Sarah, and their mother, Rita. He also asked for comfort to fall upon Hank as he came into the last parts of his life. As he finished praying, David held within him a sense of how fragile life truly is and how valuable each moment really is. Leaving his driveway, he decided to call Tyler on his way to *Carlton's* that morning.

"Everything okay?" Tyler inquired immediately. "You don't usually call in the morning."

"I just need some prayer, Brother. I have a big work thing today and Cindy's dad was moved to hospice."

"Prayers going up for you and the family, Brother."

"Thank you. There is good news, though. My grandson was born last night. His name is Jack."

"Wow! That's great! Congratulations, David. Melody had the baby early then, I take it? Both her and her son are healthy though?"

"Yep."

"Awesome. Hey, I'm about to head into a meeting with an investor, so I have to let you go."

"Okay. Talk to you later."

Hanging up with Tyler, David stared ahead at the road as he drove to work. He desperately wanted to hop in a plane and fly out to New Hampshire. He wanted to be there for his daughter, for Jack, and for his wife, but he couldn't. He was responsible for his work at *Carlton's* and he couldn't shake it. Mark might have skipped out on their business, but David couldn't do it. Pushing all his wants and desires aside, he focused on the meeting ahead, rehearsing his presentation that would be commencing in two short hours.

WITH THE WHOLE warehouse looking at Albert and David as they stood towering on the metal walkway above the group, David wasn't listening to a single word Albert was speaking beside him. His mind was elsewhere. He was thinking about Hank, about his daughter, and about his wife. *Life is fragile, precious,* he thought to himself. His phone vibrated in his pocket. Slipping it partially out of his pocket, he saw it was a text from Tyler. He pulled it out and read it quickly. Albert suddenly tapped his shoulder, snapping David out of his thoughts.

David's mind went blank and his expression along with it.

Albert chuckled and turned to the crowd. "You gotta give us old timers a moment to collect our thoughts."

The warehouse workers all laughed.

He turned to David with a raised set of eyebrows. "You have something to say, David?"

"Yes." David's anxiety suddenly rose as the words he wanted to speak weren't the same words he had rehearsed for the last day and a half. Turning to the familiar faces that he had worked with for decades, he searched for the right words to say. Many of them had been there since the beginning of *Carlton's*. They had been there during the hard times and good. A few, he had even wept with through those difficulties.

"I'm resigning."

Everyone in the room, including Albert, gasped. Silence invaded the next few moments.

"I am handing over all control to Albert." He placed a hand on Albert's shoulder, then smiled at him and turned his attention back to the crowd. "You are all in good hands. Many of you know me enough to know this doesn't come easy. Albert has been implementing a lot of change here for the last couple of months, and I want you to know it's been for the better. As you already know, he's bringing us up to speed as a business. The big boys have been offering products online for a long time, and Albert is helping us play catch-up in that regard. These are good things, and I hope you all can continue to embrace these changes. Mark and I tried our hand at online sales but struggled."

Dean from the crowd below commented, "You mean that 'under construction' page that's been there since the 90s?"

Everyone laughed.

Holding a hand up, David smiled as he nodded in agreement. "Exactly. Albert is going to take this company to places Mark and I never conceived, and he's taking you all with him. I know many of you have struggled like I have with the changes going on, but I tell you the truth when I say this man believes in his employees. He is under the same philosophy as I am when it comes to the people who work for him. He believes in you and will take care of the employees, and they'll take care of the customers."

Albert leaned into David's ear during a pause. "I wish you would've spoken to me about this before right now."

Nodding, David shrugged. "I didn't know it was happening until right now."

Turning back to the people he had grown to love over the years, David saw faces with tears and sorrow-filled expressions. He was moved with compassion and his eyes began to water. "You've been like a family to me for decades, but it's time I transition to a new chapter in my life. I wish you all the best and I will continue to stay in contact and keep you all in my prayers."

After his talk, David left his office door open and people came by on their breaks and lunches throughout the day to wish him the best. As the day wound down, Albert walked in through the open doorway while David was signing the papers that he had dropped off to him earlier in the day.

"I'm about finished signing these. Just give me a minute."

"That's fine, but this isn't about that." Albert closed the door and came and sat down in the chair in front of David's desk. His shoulders sagged and he looked conflicted.

"Okay . . . what's on your mind?"

"First, I want to say thank you. I think it was not only

hard for you to step down, but also to hand control over to me."

"You're welcome. And the second?"

He scooted his chair a little closer to the desk and then clasped his hands together as he leaned forward in his chair. "I just found out my brother's internal organs are shutting down and he'll be dead in the next day."

"Wow. You just found out?"

He nodded and then leaned back in his chair. "You know, it's a funny thing. I have all the money in the world I could imagine, and I can pay for the best doctors too, but I can't buy peace of mind. My mortality freaks me out."

David hadn't expected this intimate moment with Albert, but he knew it was a chance to point the man to God. Rising from his desk chair, he came around to the front of the desk and knelt beside Albert. He rested a hand on his back. "Do you believe in God, Albert?"

"I've never seen Him do anything good, so no, I do not."

Right then, David wanted to stand up and walk away from the man. He was done with *Carlton's* and it'd be easy to be done with him. But a force within him he couldn't identify as anything outside of God urged him to stay and continue speaking with the man. "Well, I do believe in God, and I'd like to tell you about Him."

"I already know you believe in God. You read your Bible in *all* of your free time at work. What good would God do in this time? It's not like He's going to heal my brother."

David's heart stirred within him, pressing him forward. "Listen, you mentioned *peace* and God supplies it abundantly to those who seek Him. I know you have a lot of money, Albert, and you can do things people could only dream of, but there's more to this life than money. Let me ask you something. With all this money you have, have you ever had enough?"

He blinked and then shrugged. "It's enough to live on."

David could stop right there, but the Spirit of God inside him made him go further. "But you want more, right?"

"Well, yeah. There's always someone more successful and doing more than me. I want to get to the next level. That's called having grit and working hard! Ain't nothing wrong with that!"

"Yes, you work hard and want to achieve, and that's good. But I'm here to tell you that what you're after isn't achievement, success, or a dollar amount." A deep part of David's soul connected with his words as they rolled off his tongue. Passion overwhelmed David and he pressed a hand against his own chest. "You see, Albert, we all have a God-sized hole in our hearts . . . only *God* can fill it."

"Well, if there is a God, he knows I'm a good person."

"Let's put that to the test using God's law."

"Okay. Go ahead."

"Have you ever told a lie?"

He laughed. "Of course. Everyone has."

David smiled. "God doesn't grade on a curve, Albert. What do you call someone who tells lies?"

He was quiet a moment, and then he squinted. "A liar."

"Have you ever looked at a woman with lust?"

"Yes."

"Same here. Jesus said if you so much as look at a woman with lust, you have committed adultery. What do you call someone who commits adultery?"

"Adulterer."

"Have you ever stolen something? Even if it was small like a pen."

"Yes, but I haven't done that since I was a child and it was a candy bar."

"Okay. And what do you call someone who steals?"

"A thief."

"So, by your own words, you are a liar, adulterer, and a thief. We've only done three of God's laws. If you're in God's court of law and standing before Him, the Judge, on judgment day, are you guilty or not guilty of breaking the law?"

"But I'm sorry about it and I don't do it anymore!"

"Would being sorry get you off the hook with a judge in the court of law?"

"Well, no . . ."

"Exactly. Guilty or not guilty?"

Albert sighed heavily. "Guilty. You know, David, this is depressing."

"Wait." David beamed with a smile on his lips and in his heart. "There's good news!"

Albert's eyes widened, and he leaned toward David. "Really? What?"

"God loves you so much, Albert, that He sent His only begotten Son to die for you. Imagine the court room and you were just found guilty. Now Jesus busts open the door in the back of the court room and comes before the judge and declares He is taking the burden of the guilt onto Himself."

"Why would He do that?"

"Because, Albert, *God loves you*. He loves you so much that He sent Jesus to pay your price on Calvary's cross. He saves you from Hell, He saves me from Hell. All we have to do is accept this free gift of God."

He was quiet for a long moment. Then, Albert stood up. "I have to go."

"Wait." David thought it was going differently, and he searched for words to add to say, but he was coming up short in the moment.

Albert turned to David.

"Will you at least think about what we talked about here?"

"Yes."

"Okay. And can I pray with you for your brother?"

"Yes. You can." Albert came closer to David and he led Albert in prayer. After they prayed and Albert left, David realized that the conversation was merely a seed. He knew God was ultimately the One in control and today wasn't the day for Albert's salvation, even if that's what David wanted. *Continue to teach my heart to rely on Your timing, Lord, not my own. Amen.*

CHAPTER 28

LEAVING THE CAFETERIA IN THE evening, Cindy headed for the elevator that led up to the second floor of the hospital. As she waited for the elevator doors to open, she thought about her day with Melody, Tyson, and baby Jack. Tyson and Melody's friends from church who were watching Alice had even brought her up for a visit that afternoon to meet her new brother. The entire day was full of memories in the making. It took most of Cindy's strength not to think about the fact that David wasn't there with them. It hurt too much to think of his not being there. Between David's absence and her father's move to hospice, she was hanging on by a thread emotionally.

The elevator doors finally dinged opened.

She stepped out and headed down the reflective white floor of the hospital wing. As she came closer to the door of Melody's room, she heard a deep voice of a man inside the room. It wasn't Tyson. It took only a second for Cindy to realize who it was. Coming around the corner of the room, she smiled as she saw David sitting on the hospital bed, holding Jack in his arms. Her heart melted and her eyes instantly glistened.

Rushing over to the bed, her smile and heart warmed.

"You came!"

He looked over at her and smiled. "There's nowhere else in the world I'd rather be right now than right here with my family. Sorry it took me so long to get here."

"Oh, *David*!" Throwing her arms around her husband, her heart swelled with joy. He had come, and she loved him all the more for it.

A short while later, Cindy and David excused themselves to go grab a cup of coffee and hold hands. It had been so long since they had seen each other. On their way to the coffee maker, David explained to her how he had quit *Carlton's*.

She stopped and touched his arm as concern filled her. "But you love that company. It's your business, David."

"I know, but I love you more. I love God more."

"I don't want you to give it up for me."

"I'm not. I'm giving it up for God."

"For God?"

He nodded. "Yes. I've been holding onto *Carlton's* for too long. It was a little kingdom about me and for myself. I'm using the money from selling it to help Tyler with a shelter in Spokane he started. It's designed to help people get second chances at life, but at the same time, point them to God. Today, right before my big presentation at work, I got a text from Tyler. His very last chance for an investor fell through. He would have to shut the doors on the shelter and give up the dream. I knew exactly what I was meant to do in that moment. Between what was going on with your dad, with Melody, and with you . . . I knew exactly what the right thing to do was, and I did it. I had to give my kingdom for His kingdom and purpose. Hopefully, all of that is okay with you."

"Yes, of course I'm okay with it. That's a huge step, David. It *will* change our lives forever."

"I know." He smiled and then pulled her in for a hug. "I love you."

She nodded and embraced her husband. Though they were thousands of miles from home, she felt at home in David's embrace.

THREE DAYS LATER, David and Cindy flew to Michigan to see her father. Over the course of their time with Melody, David was teaching her and telling her about the importance of forgiveness. When the time finally came to step on the plane and fly out to her hometown, she was ready.

Heart pounding and her hand resting on that familiar golden doorknob of her childhood home, she bowed her head. *God, help me to let go. Let me not be mad when I see his face in a moment.*

She stopped and glanced back at David as he was standing at the side of their rental car. He nodded and mouthed the words, 'I love you.'

Turning, she proceeded into the house. Crossing the threshold and into the warmth, she shut the door behind her. There he was, lying on a hospital bed in the middle of the living room. Her heart broke for her father as she came closer. His eyes were closed, and hospice nurses were administering medication into his IV. Her mother caught her attention from the open doorway into the kitchen and motioned her over.

Cindy's eyes couldn't leave her father's face though. She was surprised to feel no anger or animosity, only compassion and heartache. Finally able, Cindy moved from the living room and to the kitchen where her mother was waiting for her.

"Mom . . ."

"Oh, Cindy!" Throwing her arms around Cindy, Rita wept. Hearing her mother's strained words and sobbing caused Cindy to cry along with her. Holding each other for a few minutes, they didn't exchange words, only tears.

Finally releasing from their embrace, Rita grabbed a tissue box from the counter and took a few before offering the box to Cindy. She took a couple and dabbed her cheeks and eyes.

"I can't believe he's dying, Mom. He was just fine when Sarah talked to him a week ago!"

Rita's gaze rested on the hospital bed a few feet away as she nodded. *"I know . . ."*

"A part of me is so mad at him, Mom. He has missed out on so much!"

"I'm mad too." Rita shook her head. "He thought he had more time though. He thought there was time to make things right between the two of you. He doesn't want you to hate him. He loves you."

"Mom, I don't hate him for what he did. I feel bad for everything he has missed because of it. His grandchildren will never know him now."

They wept and embraced again. Interrupting their moment together, a nurse came close to the two of them.

"He's up but I'm not sure for how long."

Rita nodded to Cindy and then looked toward the hospital bed. "Go see him. Your sister already did."

"Where is she, by the way?"

"She ran to get some food. She'll be back. Stop delaying. Go see him."

Cindy's heart pounded as she nodded and then made her way over to her dying father's bedside. Peering into his eyes, her heart crumbled.

"Daddy . . ."

His lips trembled and his eyes watered. "I'm so sorry, Cindy."

Her heart was warmed with his love and she came closer, resting her head against his chest. "I love you, Dad."

It wasn't long before he slipped back into his medically-induced sleep. They had her father on high levels of medication to make the transition from life to death as painless as possible. David, Cindy, and Sarah all stayed at the house for the following three days until he passed away.

CHAPTER 29

Arriving back through the doorway of her home three days after the funeral, Cindy was overwhelmed with a mingled sense of peace and sadness. Her father had passed into eternity and now she was back home with David. She knew as she traveled through the house that it had been far too long since she had been home. Conviction of her wrongdoing plagued her thoughts.

Cindy took her and David's suitcases to the laundry room and she started in on laundry. She wanted to keep herself distracted from thoughts of her father and the conviction she was feeling at the moment. Filling the washer, she opened the cupboard to find her detergent. It wasn't there. Opening the cupboard beside it, she didn't find it there either. Frustration leaking into her current state, she went out into the living room to find David.

"Where's the detergent? Or are we out?"

"Oh, I moved it to the side of the washer. It's on the floor."

Furrowing her eyebrows, she shook her head as she crossed her arms. "Why on earth would you put it there?"

David seemed to recognize her uneasiness through her harshness over something trivial, so he set his Bible down and stood up from the couch. He grabbed her hands gently and looked at her with loving eyes.

"*Honey,*" he said softly. "I just liked it there since most of the dirty clothes ended up in a pile while you were gone. That's all."

His understanding demeanor didn't shake her mood. She lashed out in her response. "That's the stupidest thing I've ever heard of."

Jerking her hands away from him, she went back to the laundry room. Cindy knew her anger wasn't justified in the slightest and she felt uncomfortable within her own skin. As she closed the lid of the washer, she clenched her eyes shut and prayed. *God, what is wrong with me? Help me, Lord.* As she lingered in the quiet, she thought about the detergent. *He has learned to live without me.* The thought stung, and she knew she needed to repair the damage from moments earlier with David. She returned to the living room.

"Honey?"

He turned on the couch, looking directly at her. "Yes?"

"I'm sorry."

"For what?"

Her anger returned instantly. "For what? Are you kidding?"

And just like that, she was angry again. Cindy's willpower over her own emotions was weak. Coming over to the couch, she sat down beside David. "I'm sorry. I keep feeling so angry. I'm upset. I can't control it."

David turned toward her on the couch and grabbed her hands gently, his expression in his eyes still soft. "What's going on in your heart?"

"I . . . I don't like the fact that you learned how to live

without me. I don't like that my dad is dead. I don't like that my daughter and grandchildren moved across the country."

He was quiet, his expression still soft, concern evident in his eyes.

"You are so different, David."

"I'm sorry." His words were laced with grief.

"No, it's good. The problem is *me*. I don't know how to push out all the bad in my heart. I haven't been working on my relationship with God like you have. I feel weak and stuck and broken."

Her husband was quiet for a few moments. Then, softly and with a loving tone, he asked, "Can I say something?"

She nodded. "Please do."

"If you don't feel like you've been working on your relationship with God, I get that. You've been busy with your sister, your art, and your dad. But love, you can start now."

His words calmed the raging war inside and gave hope to Cindy. "That's true, I can. Where do I start?"

Reaching over to the coffee table, he grabbed his Bible and handed it to her. "The Word of God. The biggest thing I've learned through all this is learning to have my dependence on Him. He desires for us to rely on Him and even though I had been going to church for a long time . . ." David paused for a moment. "The biggest thing I learned was I need to rely on God every day and all day. He sustains my life and carries my very breath in His hands. My life is in His control. I'm far from perfect and I won't ever be until I get out of my sinful body and into my Heavenly one, but until then, I will strive to please my Heavenly Father. I've learned it's not about the pain and hurt that people put us through. It's about our relationship with Him. When I keep in mind the Cross and what Jesus did there, I am unable to be prideful, arrogant, un-thankful, or even focused on myself for a second.

Keeping my eyes on what God did for all of us is key to everything."

Processing her husband's words as she smoothed a hand over the leather front of the Bible, Cindy knew her husband was leading her in the right direction. After a long moment processing, she peered up at her husband again.

"Thank you for not giving up on me."

"Thank God, not me. It's by His power and grace I am here—we are here—in this moment together."

"How did you do it?"

He shook his head. "What?"

"Forgive me."

"God revealed to me that forgiving you doesn't make what happened okay. You remember that parable Jesus told about the servant who owed a ton of money to his master and it was forgiven?"

"Yes."

"I did some research and it turns out to be in the *billions* if it were modern-day. Anyway, *I'm* that servant. I owe God everything, Cindy, and I could never come close to paying Him back for the salvation He has given me. When He forgave me, He forgave any wrong done toward me. You see? I am forgiven and that forgiveness flows through me and toward you."

Seeing her husband's face warm with joy and eyes filled with tears of sincerity moved a deep part of her. She desired to experience God the way David had experienced Him, and she was overwhelmed with a spiritual thirst in her soul.

"Okay. I'm going to go read for a while." Rising to her feet, Cindy clutched her husband's Bible tightly and held it against her chest, heading for the bedroom for time with God.

. . .

THAT EVENING, Cindy made the two of them dinner. Her time in God's Word had done her soul good. She hadn't ever read the Bible for more than a few minutes at a time, and earlier that day, she had taken in two full hours of God's Word. When she finished, she had felt like her world was changed, and it was, for she had spent real time with God. She now carried within her a calmness that she hadn't experienced in her life in quite some time. It was as if the Word of God had renewed life in her dry bones.

Setting the plates of Alfredo down on their table, Cindy went out front and beckoned David from shoveling snow in the driveway.

He came in and hung up his jacket in the closet and left his shoes by the front door. As he walked into the dining room to sit down, she smiled as her gaze stayed fixed on the man she loved.

"You're an amazing man, David. You know that?"

David smiled and took a seat in a chair at the table. "You're not too bad yourself." He winked at her and then his eyes fell to his plate of food. "Oh, how I have missed your home cooking. I might've changed the detergent's location and a few other things around here, but I never did figure out how to cook a decent meal."

She smiled. "Well, you won't ever have to worry about that again. Now that you mention it, I want to say sorry again. I can't seem to forgive myself for what I've done to you."

He smiled. "Dear, it's not your job to forgive yourself. That's the responsibility of Jesus Christ, and He already has. As for me, I forgive you, but a part of me is glad it all happened. God has taught me so much in your time away. I might have lost my wife for a couple of months, but what I gained was a real relationship with God. I no longer see the world through my limited humanistic and selfish view but through the eyes of God Himself."

"I hope my being here won't change that now."

He shook his head as he folded his hands. "It won't. I could never go backward from this. Let's thank God for this food and eat. I'm starving." They bowed their heads and David led them in a prayer.

CHAPTER 30

A MONTH LATER, THE SHELTER opened its doors and both David and Cindy helped feed the homeless who showed up for a hot bowl of soup that first night. David worked by handing out bowls of soup and Cindy, along with her sister Sarah, who had flown out for a visit, helped by handing people drinks and napkins. Jonathan and Charlie, along with their wives, were also there helping feed people. Some were handing out rolls and others were greeting people as they came through the door. Tyler was busy making sure everything was flowing smoothly and checking in with each volunteer station.

February was exceptionally chilly for Spokane this year, and the rooms filled within twenty minutes of opening. It brought David's heart joy to see so many people willing to take the second chance at life, and his eyes watered as he watched one woman in particular sign in at the table. She had a small boy next to her at the table. He couldn't have been much older than two years of age. Seeing the mother busy with paperwork, David went over and bent his knees.

"Hi, little man. What's your name?"

"Jack."

He smiled. "I have a grandson named Jack. That's a pretty cool name."

Shy, the boy shifted behind his mother's legs.

"Hi. Sorry about that." The woman glanced over at David as she paused filling out the paperwork. "He is a little shy."

"It's okay." David stood up and introduced himself.

She nodded and shook his hand. "I'm Chloe. Jack and I just lost everything we own in a house fire a week ago. Last month, Jack lost his father. It's been a rough little while for us."

Moved with compassion, David frowned. "I'm so sorry to hear that. God brought you to the right place. Tyler has a heart for this, and he'll help you get back on your feet."

Smiling she said, "Thanks. It's a blessing you guys have opened this place up."

"By the will of God, it happened. I'd better get back to work. It was nice meeting you, Chloe."

Nodding, she turned back to the forms and continued filling them out.

As the evening progressed, David heard more stories like Chloe's. People who had fallen into hard times who were not only desperate for help but open to the idea of God. David knew this shelter Tyler had decided to take on wasn't just a place to fill a need in the homeless community of Spokane but a real chance to share God's love with people through His people.

After all the new residents were in their rooms and the last person who was eating left, Cindy slipped away to go help with dishes in the kitchen with Olivia. Tyler and David sat down at one of the tables.

"That went well," Tyler remarked as he let out a sigh and surveyed the room where an hour ago, there were over a hundred people sitting and eating. A moment passed and then he looked over at David. "You've been a Godsend, Brother. I couldn't have done this all without you."

"You had a lot done before I really got involved."

He shook his head. "No way, man. I was struggling to see how it was all going to come together until you swooped in and saved the day."

"You can thank God for that, Tyler. And thank you for having us as part of the team. I think that this is a great third act for Cindy and me, and we can all be blessed by it."

Checking over his shoulder, Tyler sat up and leaned in a little closer as his voice lowered. "Things with the lady still going well?"

"Yes, they are. She's been seeking the Lord and finding joy in serving here and at our church. I've come to realize something over this last month since she's been home. I used to think I was in control of my life years ago. I seriously thought I had everything under control and together . . . but I never did." David laughed, thinking about his immaturity of thought and security back when he was really getting *Carlton's* up and running. "It wasn't until I lost all my perceived control and surrendered myself fully to God that I realized I never had control to begin with. Once I realized that, I was able to start seeing my wife for who she really is, a sinner saved by grace and forgiven by God. Nothing about that has a thing to do with me. It's all God."

"It makes sense. God doesn't want us thinking we have a hand in any of this. It's all His and for His glory."

"That's right. Because if we believe we are the ones who are due the credit, He doesn't get the glory, we do. That's worship of self. That's modern-day idolatry."

Cindy's face popped into David's view as she leaned through the kitchen window opening. David smiled as he caught her gaze. She smiled back. He loved that woman and that had never stopped. He used to think it was her sin of the past that had crippled him, but in fact, it had been himself that crippled him. It had been his disjointed relationship with the Lord. Now that he had discovered the truth and the beauty of God through his trials, David knew he could love his wife the way God had always intended.

The End.

BOOK PREVIEWS

LOVE'S RETURN PREVIEW

Prologue

THE FIRST TIME I LAID eyes on Kirk was back in our senior year of High School while I was walking the track with Chloe. He was beneath the bleachers lip-locked with Vicky Haggar from the cheerleading squad. This wouldn't have been an issue outside of the fact that he was dating my best-friend, Chloe. Not exactly a best first impression.

Two years later when I was twenty, I decided to relocate from Albany, New York, to Spokane, Washington. Kirk had found out about the big journey across country through mutual friends and approached me about road tripping together. I quickly rejected him. When he offered to pay for all the gas, I couldn't help but give in. With over 2,000 miles to reach Spokane and a strong desire not to rely on my parents anymore, I knew his gas money would help me in the long run. I was on my way to Spokane to stake a claim in my independence from my parents and to work at a software company as a receptionist. Kirk had been into hockey and hoped for a chance at the big leagues by trying out for the Spokane Chiefs.

Through the long journey across the country, somewhere between Buffalo and Cleveland, I suspect, Kirk and I became friends. During our time together on the road, we laughed about Mrs. Bovey, our ninth-grade English teacher who hated children far too much to be teaching them in a school. We also shared our hopes and desires for the future.

When we finally arrived in Spokane five days after we left our hometown, I not only had a handful of memories from our road trip but a longing for something more for *us*. The trip had given me a chance to see past the façade he had put on in high school and see the real Kirk. At one stop along the way, at a gas station out in the middle of nowhere, he opened my car door for me. Then another time, he grabbed me my favorite candy bar without my even having to ask. When I became tired of driving, he'd willingly take over even if he was tired. Beyond those sweet gestures, I learned of a man who held a lot of regret over his checkered past. He had high hopes to start afresh and make a new life for himself in Spokane. Beneath all the muscles, I found a man with a big heart.

I couldn't give into my desire to see him again, though, or to possibly have a relationship. He was, after all, Chloe's ex-boyfriend. I dropped him off at the bus stop where his friend was picking him up and said goodbye for what I thought was forever.

Chapter 1-Jessica

FIVE YEARS AND TWO JOBS later, I was on my way to work when I stopped in at a favorite local coffee shop of mine downtown, Milo's, for an extra boost of caffeine. I had already been running late for work as it was, sleeping through all three of my alarms. There was a reason to the madness. It was all due to my friend Isabella, who had kept me up half the night on the phone. She was like me, single and living on the hopes of someday being swept away by a gallant gentleman who would show us the love we needed. We talked last night about how miserable she was being single in a world full of married men, the only single ones being creeps. I understood the pain of loneliness, but only to a certain degree. My singleness was part of who I was. It had almost become a friend. Sure, I wanted someone to love and hold, but I had to trust the fact that God was in control and knew my heart. Plus, I had my work, which filled much of my time.

Standing in the coffee shop near the counter, I waited for my order. I had on my new white pea coat I had just picked up the other day at the mall. When I saw it hanging on the rack on my way through Macy's, I instantly fell in love with it. It went perfectly with my red bucket hat, which I was also wearing. Scrolling through emails on my phone as I waited for my coffee, I felt the pressure of the day catching up with me. Already several new messages. Two from Micah, my boss, one from the graphics department on a design mock-up, and a reply from a pastor I had interviewed a couple of months back. Working at a startup magazine was anything but easy, but I loved every second of it. Not only was I a writer and reporter, but my boss, Micah's, go-to person for whatever he needed. Sometimes, it meant donuts and coffee on my way into work, and sometimes, it meant writing ten articles in five days and spot-checking the print run at two o'clock in the morning, four hours before it went to print. It was hard work, but it carried purpose and I thrived on purpose.

"Kirk," the barista said behind the counter, setting a cup down.

It took a moment for the name to register in my mind,

but when it did, my heart leapt as I lifted my eyes to find the face that went with the name. I didn't think about him often, but when he did brush across my thoughts, it was always with fondness for the time we'd shared together on the car trip five years ago. Over the years, the man had stayed with me in the depths of my soul, along with regret. Regret over the fact I hadn't pursued him the day I dropped him off at the bus stop. We hadn't spent time together before our car ride, but the time we did share over the trip was something special and close to my heart still to this day.

Surveying the coffee shop, I held onto the short string of hope I had carried all these years. It was like a loose thread from a piece of clothing that I knew if I pulled, it would unravel the whole thing. I refused to part with it. There was no certainty that Kirk still lived in Spokane, but it didn't stop me from holding onto the possibility. My friend Chloe, back in Albany, hadn't spoken his name in years, understandably, and I'd never found his name on the Spokane Chiefs' roster (I checked every season), but still . . . I refused to part with the string.

"Thanks," a man said, his voice rugged, worn.

Did you enjoy this sample? Pick it up on Amazon today!

ONE THURSDAY MORNING PREVIEW

Prologue

To love and be loved—it was all I ever wanted. Nobody could ever convince me John was a bad man. He made me feel loved when I did not know what love was. I was his and he was mine. It was perfect . . . or at least, I thought it was.

I cannot pinpoint why everything changed in our lives, but it did—and for the worst. My protector, my savior, and my whole world came crashing down like a heavy spring downpour. The first time he struck me, I remember thinking it was just an accident. He had been drinking earlier in the day with his friends and came stumbling home late that night. The lights were low throughout the house because I had already gone to bed. I remember hearing the car pull up outside in the driveway. Leaping to my feet, I came rushing downstairs and through the kitchen to greet him. He swung, which I thought at the time was because I startled him, and the back side of his hand caught my cheek.

I should have known it wasn't an accident.

The second time was no accident at all, and I knew it. After a heavy night of drinking the night his father died, he came to the study where I was reading. Like a hunter looking for his prey, he came up behind me to the couch. Grabbing the back of my head and digging his fingers into my hair, he kinked my neck over the couch and asked me why I hadn't been faithful to him. I had no idea what he was talking about, so out of sheer fear, I began to cry. John took that as a sign of guilt and backhanded me across the face. It was hard enough to leave a bruise the following day. I stayed with him anyway. I'd put a little extra makeup on around my eyes or anywhere else when marks were left. I didn't stay because I was stupid, but because I loved him. I kept telling myself that our love could get us through this. The night of his father's death, I blamed his outburst on the loss of his father. It was too much for him to handle, and he was just letting out steam. I swore to love him through the good times and the bad. This was just one of the bad times.

Each time he'd hit me, I'd come up with a reason or excuse for the behavior. There was always a reason, at least in my mind, as to why John hit me. Then one time, after a really bad injury, I sought help from my mother before she passed away. The closest thing to a saint on earth, she dealt with my father's abuse for decades before he died. She was a devout Christian, but a warped idea of love plagued my mother her entire life. She told me, 'What therefore God hath joined together, let not man put asunder.' That one piece of advice she gave me months before passing made me suffer through a marriage with John for another five trying years.

Each day with John as a husband was a day full of prayer. I would pray for him not to drink, and sometimes, he didn't —those were the days I felt God had listened to my pleas. On the days he came home drunk and swinging, I felt alone, like God had left me to die by my husband's hands. Fear was a cornerstone of our relationship, in my eyes, and I hated it. As the years piled onto one another, I began to deal with two entirely different people when it came to John. There was the John who would give me everything I need in life and bring flowers home on the days he was sober, and then there was John, the drunk, who would bring insults and injury instead of flowers.

I knew something needed to desperately change in my life, but I didn't have the courage. Then one day, it all changed when two little pink lines told me to run and never look back.

Chapter 1

Fingers glided against the skin of my arm as I lay on my side looking into John's big, gorgeous brown eyes. It was morning, so I knew he was sober, and for a moment, I thought maybe, just maybe I could tell him about the baby growing inside me. Flashes of a shared excitement between us blinked through my mind. He'd love having a baby around the house. *He really would.* Behind those eyes, I saw the man I fell in love with years ago down in Town Square in New York City. Those eyes were the same ones that brought me into a world of love and security I had never known before. Moments like that made it hard to hate him. Peering over at his hand that was tracing the side of my body, I saw the cut on his knuckles from where he had smashed the coffee table a few nights ago. My heart retracted the notion of telling him about the baby. I knew John would be dangerous for a child.

Chills shivered up my spine as his fingers traced from my arm to the curve of my back. *Could I be strong enough to live without him?* I wondered as the fears sank back down into me. Even if he was a bit mean, he had a way of charming me like no other man I had ever met in my life. He knew how to touch gently, look deeply and make love passionately. It was only when he drank that his demons came out.

"Want me to make you some breakfast?" I asked, slipping out of his touch and from the bed to my feet. His touches were enjoyable, but I wanted to get used to not having them. My mind often jumped back and forth between leaving, not leaving, and something vaguely in between. It was hard.

John smiled up at me from the bed with what made me feel like love in his eyes. I suddenly began to feel bad about the plan to leave, but I knew he couldn't be trusted with a child. *Keep it together.*

"Sure, babe. That'd be great." He brought his muscular arms from out of the covers and put them behind his head. My eyes traced his biceps and face. Wavy brown hair and a jawline that was defined made him breathtakingly gorgeous. Flashes of last night's passion bombarded my mind. He didn't drink, and that meant one thing—we made love. It started in the main living room just off the foyer. I was enjoying my evening cup of tea while the fireplace was lit when suddenly, John came home early. I was worried at first, but when he leaned over the couch and pulled back my blonde hair, he planted a tender kiss on my neck. I knew right in that moment that it was going to be a good night. Hoisting me up from the couch with those arms and pressing me against the wall near the fireplace, John's passion fell from his lips and onto the skin of my neck as I wrapped my arms around him.

The heat between John and me was undeniable, and it made the thoughts of leaving him that much harder. It was during those moments of pure passion that I could still see the bits of the John I once knew—the part of John that didn't scare me and had the ability to make me feel safe, and the part of him that I never wanted to lose.

"All right," I replied with a smile as I broke away from my thoughts. Leaving down the hallway, I pushed last night out of my mind and focused on the tasks ahead.

Retrieving the carton of eggs from the fridge in the kitchen, I shut the door and was startled when John was standing on the other side. Jumping, I let out a squeak. "John!"

He tilted his head and slipped closer to me. With nothing on but his boxer briefs, he backed me against the counter and let his hand slide the corner of my shirt up my side. He leaned closer to me. I felt the warmth of his breath on my skin as my back arched against the counter top. He licked his lips instinctively to moisten them and then gently let them find their way to my neck. "Serenah . . ." he said in a smooth, seductive voice.

"Let me make you breakfast," I said as I set the carton down on the counter behind me and turned my neck into him to stop the kissing.

His eyebrows rose as he pulled away from my body and released. His eyes met mine. There it was—the change. "*Fine.*"

"What?" I replied as I turned and pulled down a frying pan that hung above the island counter.

"Nothing. Nothing. I have to go shower." He left down the hallway without a word, but I could sense tension in his tone.

Waiting for the shower to turn on after he walked into the bathroom and slammed the door, I began to cook his eggs. When a few minutes had passed and I hadn't heard the water start running, I lifted my eyes and looked down the hallway.

There he was.

John stood at the end of hallway, watching me. Standing in the shifting shadows of the long hallway, he was more than creepy. He often did that type of thing, but it came later in the marriage, not early on and only at home. I never knew how long he was standing there before I caught him, but he'd always break away after being seen. He had a sick obsession of studying me like I was some sort of weird science project of his.

I didn't like it all, but it was part of who he had become. *Not much longer,* I reminded myself.

I smiled down the hallway at him, and he returned to the bathroom to finally take his shower. As I heard the water come on, I finished the eggs and set the frying pan off the burner. Dumping the eggs onto a plate, I set the pan in the sink and headed to the piano in the main living room. Pulling the bench out from under the piano, I got down on my hands and knees and lifted the flap of carpet that was squared off. Removing the plank of wood that concealed my secret area, I retrieved the metal box and opened it.

Freedom.

Ever since he hit me that second time, a part of me knew we'd never have the forever marriage I pictured, so in case I was right, I began saving money here and there. I had been able to save just over ten thousand dollars. A fibbed high-priced manicure here, a few non-existent shopping trips with friends there. It added up, and John had not the foggiest clue, since he was too much of an egomaniac to pay attention to anything that didn't directly affect him. Sure, it was his money, but money wasn't really 'a thing' to us. We were beyond that. My eyes looked at the money in the stash and then over at the bus ticket to Seattle dated for four days from now. I could hardly believe it. I was really going to finally leave him after all this time. Amongst the cash and bus ticket, there was a cheap pay-as-you go cellphone and a fake ID. I had to check that box at least once a day ever since I found out about my pregnancy to make sure he hadn't found it. I was scared to leave, but whenever I felt that way, I rubbed my pregnant thirteen-week belly, and I knew I had to do what was best for *us*. Putting the box back into the floor, I was straightening out the carpet when suddenly, John's breathing settled into my ears behind me.

"What are you doing?" he asked, towel draped around his waist behind me. *I should have just waited until he left for work . . . What were you thinking, Serenah?* My thoughts scolded me.

Slamming my head into the bottom of the piano, I grabbed my head and backed out as I let out a groan. "There was a crumb on the carpet."

"What? Underneath the piano?" he asked.

Anxiety rose within me like a storm at sea. Using the bench for leverage, I placed a hand on it and began to get up. When I didn't respond to his question quick enough, he shoved my arm that was propped on the piano bench, causing me to smash my eye into the corner of the bench. Pain radiated through my skull as I cupped my eye and began to cry.

"Oh, please. That barely hurt you."

I didn't respond. Falling the rest of the way to the floor, I cupped my eye and hoped he'd just leave. Letting out a heavy sigh, he got down, still in his towel, and put his hand on my shoulder. "I'm sorry, honey."

Jerking my shoulder away from him, I replied, "Go away!"

He stood up and left.

John hurt me sober? Rising to my feet, I headed into the half-bathroom across the living room and looked into the mirror. My eye was blood red—he had popped a blood vessel. Tears welled in my eyes as my eyebrows furrowed in disgust.

Four days wasn't soon enough to leave—I was leaving today.

FREE GIFT

Cole has fought hundreds of fires in his lifetime, but he had never tasted fear until he came to fighting a fire in his own home. *Amongst The Flames* is a Christian firefighter fiction that tackles real-life situations and problems that exist in Christian marriages today. It brings with it passion, love and spiritual depth that will leave you feeling inspired. This Inspirational Christian romance novel is one book that you'll want to read over and over again.

To Claim Visit:
offer.tkchapin.com

ALSO BY T.K. CHAPIN

A Reason To Love Series

A Reason To Live

A Reason To Believe

A Reason To Forgive

Journey Of Love Series

Journey Of Grace

Journey Of Hope

Journey Of Faith

Protected By Love Series

Love's Return (Book 1)

Love's Promise (Book 2)

Love's Protection (Book 3)

Diamond Lake Series

One Thursday Morning (Book 1)

One Friday Afternoon (Book 2)

One Saturday Evening (Book 3)

One Sunday Drive (Book 4)

One Monday Prayer (Book 5)

One Tuesday Lunch (Book 6)

One Wednesday Dinner (Book 7)

Embers & Ashes Series

Amongst the Flames (Book 1)

Out of the Ashes (Book 2)

Up in Smoke (Book 3)

After the Fire (Book 4)

Love's Enduring Promise Series

The Perfect Cast (Book 1)

Finding Love (Book 2)

Claire's Hope (Book 3)

Dylan's Faith (Book 4)

Stand Alones

Love Interrupted

Love Again

A Chance at Love

The Broken Road

If Only

Because Of You

The Lies We Believe

In His Love

When It Rains

Gracefully Broken

Please join T.K. Chapin's Mailing List to be notified of upcoming releases and promotions.

Join the List

ACKNOWLEDGMENTS

First and foremost, I want to thank God. God's salvation through the death, burial and resurrection of Jesus Christ gives us all the ability to have a personal relationship with the Creator of the Universe.

I also want to thank my wife. She's my muse and my inspiration. A wonderful wife, an amazing mother and the best person I have ever met. She's great and has always stood by me with every decision I have made along life's way.

I'd like to thank my editors and early readers for helping me along the way. I also want to thank all of my friends and extended family for the support. It's a true blessing to have every person I know in my life.

ABOUT THE AUTHOR

T.K. CHAPIN writes Christian Romance books designed to inspire and tug on your heart strings. He believes that telling stories of faith, love and family help build the faith of Christians and help non-believers see how God can work in the life of believers. He gives all credit for his writing and storytelling ability to God. The majority of the novels take place in and around Spokane, Washington, his hometown. Chapin makes his home in Idaho and has the pleasure of raising his daughter and two sons with his beautiful wife Crystal.

facebook.com/officialtkchapin

twitter.com/tkchapin

instagram.com/tkchapin

Made in the USA
Middletown, DE
29 November 2019